Mel, Mikal & The Magic Trees

Author: Cee Bennett-Carayol

PB ISBN 978-0-9934193-0-0

(Black & White Interior)

Book cover artwork - Damel Senghan Carayol

Book cover graphics - Jeremy Salmon

Other graphics - Rafal Szypniewski

Main photography - Winston O. Rogers

Other photography & images: C. Bennett-Carayol, Dreamstime & J. A. Mason

Dedications

Mel, Mikal & The Magic Trees

This début novel is dedicated primarily to my lovely grandsons Nicholas and Ramel and my children, who were all part of the initial source of inspiration for this novel. It is also dedicated to the memory of my dad, other family members and previous in-laws who have passed on; all of whom were very much loved and respected.

❧Acknowledgements❧

Thanks to:

*Professional Graphic Designer Jeremy Salmon from Wedesign, who skilfully finalised the book cover and created the promotional banners.

*Talented Artist Damel Senghan Carayol for the time and effort invested in creating the fantastic, detailed artwork for the book cover that surpassed my expectations, and the support given in the early stages of writing this book.

*My husband Winston Rogers - a talented and skilled Photographer - for the amazing photos incorporated in the novel that captured my thoughts precisely and his continuous, positive encouragement.

*Rafal Szypniewski, a talented up and coming Graphic Designer for giving up his busy schedule to contribute to some of the graphics.

*My daughter Makeda, who read the first few chapters, helped with the naming of the tree characters and some of the proof reading.

*My sons Rhemie and Chad, who over the years have encouraged me to get on with the novel and get it published.

*My sister Dorothy, who took the time to read the novel in its entirety in the draft, infancy stages; and my friend Ricky Denton who did the same and continued to support and compliment my efforts.

The support given from everyone was a great source of motivation that will extend to the completion of the sequel.

❧CONTENTS❧

Chapter 1: The Wishing

Mel strolled through his grandparents' garden on a warm day in the month of June; admiring the tall Ash tree in the far corner, and the slinky branches of the trees in the neighbouring garden, adorning the fence.

It was such a beautiful garden, temporarily a bit unkempt; but this had no effect on its peaceful, relaxing atmosphere and the gentle breeze rustling through the branches of the surrounding trees.

He listened to the creaking sound of the old swing pushed into movement by the breeze and resisted the urge to ride it to its heights, before gazing thoughtfully at the trees in the neighbours' garden.

It wasn't because they stood so tall and erect or, because their leaves shone in the dazzling sunlight why he found them so intriguing. Instead, it was the fact that he had a strange feeling that there were more to these trees, swaying so effortlessly in the breeze than he could see. Something puzzling that he couldn't quite figure out.

The night before, he had woken up startled by a strange dream. He couldn't remember it fully, but he knew it was about a very odd-looking tree that alarmingly attempted to chat with him. As he thought about this, he perhaps started to imagine the impossible.

'Oh I wish these trees could talk like us humans. If they could, I would ask them why they grow so tall and bend so easily with the wind.'

'Well never mind the trees,' said a rather frustrated Grandma Cee. 'Just look at the state of my lovely garden; the lawn, the overgrown shrubs ... it's beginning to look like a forest out here.'

Grandpa Dee came out to see what the fuss was all about on such a lovely day. 'Don't worry Cee,' he said calmly. 'When the new lawn mower arrives, you have my word that it will be sorted.'

Grandma Cee was slender with light brown complexion and eyes that matched her dark brown hair. In comparison, Grandpa Dee was tall and dark with similar eyes and had a tendency to dress like the younger generation despite his age.

'I really, really wish I could talk to those trees Grandma,' Mel repeated. 'If I could, I'd ask them to use their strong branches to help you clean up the lawn.'

His Aunty Keda wasn't sure if he was joking or serious. 'Don't be silly,' she said, flashing her dark brown eyes, set against her flawless chocolate, brown skin. 'Trees can't clean up the lawn; they're more likely to clutter the place with fallen leaves. And, come to think of it,' she said leaning back on the garden bench, 'when have you ever heard of a talking tree?'

An amused Grandma Cee looked at Keda, remembering an incident some years ago in the garden of their previous home in Wembley. One day, whilst cutting the shrubs and pruning the cherry blossom tree, a young Keda covered her ears and yelled, 'Stop, stop it please! You're hurting them ... the trees, the plants they are in pain!'

Grandma Cee reflected on how puzzled she felt then as she looked at Keda's petrified expression, reflected in her beautiful Egyptian shaped eyes. How can a tree or plant possibly feel pain for goodness sake? She had never heard such nonsense, and now how uncanny that many years later, her grandson in his naivety wishes he could talk to trees.

Her eyes shifted back to Mel as she thought; *now here is another deluded soul, who is certainly letting his imagination run wild- talking to trees indeed!*

Mel was a very clever nine year old with a memory like a microchip. His hair had a tendency to roll up in cute black curls and his brown skin glowed in the sunlight as he smiled; showing off a row of pearly white teeth and dimpled cheeks.

Grandma Cee often proudly imagined Mel, who loved to argue a point, as a future lawyer. However, she didn't dismiss the thought that he could become a talented singer or artist like his Grandpa Dee, who could expresses both his creative and academic side.

Similar to his dad, Grandpa Dee enjoyed passing on his knowledge to his grandchildren 'Grandpa,' said Mel. 'What type of trees are those in the garden next door?'

'Well, let's see now,' he replied, 'the one to your left is an English Elm and the other a Silver Birch.' He paused for a moment to clear his throat before patiently continuing. 'Birch trees exist in different colours, yellow, white, grey etc., but if you ask my opinion, the graceful Silver Birch, with its silvery bark and slender trunk is the finest of them all.'

He paused again. 'Now as for Elm trees, there are about forty different types, but I prefer the one you are looking at, the beautiful English Elm with its oval-shaped, jagged edged leaves - it can grow up to 100 feet tall.'

'100 feet tall! That's really, really tall,' said Mel.

As Mel listened to his Grandpa's description of the Elm and Birch trees, his fascination for trees grew even more. 'I love trees. What was your favourite tree in The Gambia Grandpa?'

'Oh I liked a lot of trees back then, but if I had to choose, it would be the mango tree; tall, strong and majestic, bearing my favourite fruit.'

'Oh lord ... did you just mention mangoes? They are my favourite too,' said Grandma Cee. 'In Jamaica, where I come from, mango trees grew everywhere. Boy let me tell you,' she said, smiling as she reflected on her childhood years and visualised the images. 'As a child I ate mangoes every day when they were in season and scoffed them like sweets.'

'All that talk about mangoes is making me hungry. What's for lunch Cee? Would you like some help?'

'Yes thanks, but after I clean up with that noisy hoover.' Grandpa Dee rolled his eyes and looked to the sky.

'It's a vacuum cleaner Cee, not a hoover ... that's the brand, why don't you say it right?'

Grandma Cee gave him such a stern look above her glasses, he stopped in mid-sentence and left the garden for a stroll, whilst Aunty Keda on leave from university, retreated to the comfort of her room.

The garden suddenly fell silent. Mel found himself looking curiously at the Birch and Elm trees once again. He felt dwarfed against their great height but yet, admired their sturdy branches; fully decked with glimmering leaves, spreading across the fence.

'Come on, talk to me,' he whispered. 'I know you can hear me.'

He waited, hoping for some sort of response but to his disappointment, nothing happened. His focus soon shifted to the atmosphere.

The gentle breeze that caressed his face earlier, strangely began to feel very gusty in comparison. He disliked strong winds. Such force he reflected, made him feel defenceless and in need of support to maintain his balance. Quite suddenly, he heard a nearby sound - a creaking sound that shook the ground a little. He turned around quickly to locate its source.

'Who's there?' he said nervously, but he had no response.

The pace of the gusty wind grew stronger and the mysterious creaking sound echoed through the air like a ship's stern, bracing itself against a storm. Mel shifted from one leg to the next and wiped off the beads of sweat forming on his brow.

He attempted to call out again, 'Who's there?' but to his surprise, only a croaking sound escaped from his lips.

All this uneasiness made him feel a sudden urge to want to pee. He crossed his legs as the thought surfaced, and then to his relief, heard his Grandma's voice in the distance.

'Mel, it's going to rain. Come on in before you get drenched.'

'Ok Grandma,' he said shakily, whilst scanning his

surroundings for the source of the sound that alarmed him somewhat. He cautiously moved backwards towards the patio door, looking sharply to his left and then to his right; wishing he had some form of defence.

A drop of rain fell on his forehead, followed by another and another, and the distant rumble of thunder, mingled with the unidentified, creaking sound suddenly made him jump.

He gasped, and ran as fast as he could through the patio door; slamming it shut to seal out all intruders; and, for a while, felt very relieved to be safe inside.

Hi There!

The patio door opened up into the dining room and adjoining kitchen, with entrance to the living room. Grandma Cee liked the living room to be kept neat, so knowing this; Mel took off his trainers and placed them neatly in the lobby area.

Still feeling shaken, he sat down to relax on the comfy, black sofa and stretched his legs on the footrest. 'Ah! I can't believe I was frightened by a bit of wind and thunder,' he muttered. 'Shame ... nearly wet myself!'

After a while, he began to feel a bit peckish. 'All I need now is a slice of Grandma's delicious carrot cake,' he said, before he remembered the rule. 'Oh man ... Grandma wouldn't be pleased if I ate this before lunch.'

He turned on the TV to watch his favourite Ben 10 programme, and quickly switched it off, as the sounds of the vacuum cleaner and Aunty Keda's music were too distracting. Feeling bored, he stared vacantly through the living room window overlooking the front lawn; hardly noticing the pitter-patter sounds of the rain on the windowsill, adding to the other distractions.

Quite unexpectedly, a new sound diverted his attention. *What's that?* he pondered. It sounds like shattering glass. 'Grandma!' he yelled, but she didn't hear him. The noisy vacuum cleaner and the sound of the R&B tune that she was humming blocked out his voice entirely.

'Aunty Keda, something crashed!' Aunty Keda was busy playing her CDs, totally oblivious to anything else going on around her.

He felt alone and a bit scared, but at the same time wanted to be responsible. 'What if it's a burglar? They might steal Grandma's pots and things,' he said to himself. 'Huh! Or, what if it's that thing - whatever it was - that made the creaking sound in the garden?'

Mel hesitated for a moment. He really didn't want to think about this again. Fear was rising in the pit of his stomach just like before, but soon, his curiosity got the better of him and he just had to find out.

He crept quietly to the dining room door and pushed it gently. Peeking through, he got such a fright he couldn't help but shriek. What he saw was absolutely, unbelievable - he was stunned.

Mel slammed the door and leant firmly against it. He could feel his heart thumping against his chest, faster than he had ever felt it before. He rubbed his eyes and blinked several times to make sure he was not dreaming -what he had just seen was very hard to accept.

The thought crossed his mind to walk away and pretend they weren't there, and perhaps they would disappear, but then he realised that the suspense was much greater than his fear. Holding his breath, he pushed the door gently, peeked through and this time he had to accept what his eyes had seen.

Seated around the table were two tree-like creatures, whom at a guess, could only be the Birch and Elm trees from next door that he had beckoned to earlier. Except now, with their ridiculous makeovers, they were a strange looking creepy pair.

Leafy faces with lips attempting a stiff smile and odd protruding eyes peered out at him. Branch arms and hands with twig-like fingers rested on their trunk laps; and large roots, positioned one above the other, took on the appearance of legs, sporting root-laced trunk boots.

Mel looked on in utter disbelief. 'Who ... who ... are you?' he managed to stutter with buckling knees. His voice then rose from a low to a high pitch. 'And what ... what ... are you doing in here?'

The dining room scene distracted him before he got an answer. What devastation! There was a huge hole in the patio door - wide enough to step through - and shattered glass with trails of mud left by the impression of the creatures' trunk boots, literally covered the floor.

Glancing outside, Mel saw that a section of the garden fence where the branches of the trees had hung so splendidly earlier was completely, wrecked. He held his trembling hands to his head in despair.

'Oh my gosh! Who ... who ... are you?' he asked again. 'What are you doing in my Grandparents' dining room? And ... and what do you want?' he managed to yell. He pictured for a split second how Grandma Cee would react to this wreckage and cringed. He knew that somehow, he just had to get them out of there.

Before answering his questions, both trees glanced at each other as if seeking confirmation for their baffled thoughts. 'Hmmm,' said the Birch tree, leaning slightly forward as he extended a branch arm to Mel and continued in a deep, resonating voice that reminded Mel of Darth Vader and transformer Optimus Prime all at once.

'Hi there, my name is Birchard and this is my good friend Elmstead.'

'It's very nice to meet you,' they said, 'how do you do?'

'Huh!' gasped a bewildered Mel. 'You can talk ... I have to get out of here, this is definitely not real!'

Birchard moved clumsily forward with puckered brow and a halo of rustling leaves to look Mel straight in the eye.

'Aaarrgh!' Mel shrieked and almost fell over as he tried to move quickly out of his reach.

'Of course we can talk!' said Birchard. 'Tell me something; didn't you wish today that we could talk so that you could ask us questions ... hmmm?'

'What! Well ... yes ... yes,' said Mel shaking uncontrollably. 'But ... but ... I didn't really think it would happen. Trees can't talk or walk. They're supposed to have roots firmly in the ground like my Biology Teacher said, not feet with root-laced boots that can crash through garden fences and patio doors.'

Mel paused, as if something had just dawned on him. 'Huh! Oh my days that eerie, creaking sound that scared me earlier was actually you two, pulling your roots out of the ground. Oh, man ... I must be dreaming! This really isn't happening!' He buried his head in his hands, trying to comprehend the reality of the situation.

'Ok! So you think you are dreaming eh ... let's see if this is true,' said Birchard. 'Let me pinch you!'

'Oh no you don't!' Mel snapped, summoning up the courage to defend himself. 'Don't touch me! Besides, those twig things aren't real fingers.'

Elmstead decided to interrupt at this point. 'Ahem, let me just add, that you should be careful what you wish for. We are after all, magic trees with the power to do whatever we wish. Well ... almost anything,' he quickly corrected himself.

'I suppose you did not realise it was your lively imagination and wish that made this possible,' said Birchard, as he leant forward and pinched Mel's nose before he could stop him.

'Ouch, how dare you!' Mel yelled. He held his nose that had suddenly turned red. 'You two had better wish that my

Grandma don't see you. You won't scare her; she will chase you out with her broomstick.'

'Chase us out with her broomstick!' the trees giggled. 'Is she pray tell, a witch?' Birchard teased.

Mel looked at him with blazing eyes. 'A witch ... you dare call my Grandma a witch!'

'Well they fly around on broomsticks don't they? You said that she would attack us with her broomstick, so what were we suppose to assume?'

'Well you thought wrong,' Mel snapped. 'Grandma said people shouldn't assume things, because they could end up looking stupid like an Ass. Come to think of it, you both look stupid right now.'

Elmstead smiled at Mel's newly emerging courage, and attempting to sit upright, bumped his leafy head on the ceiling. He winced but didn't utter a sound.

'Excuse me,' he grinned whilst rubbing his head and showing his horrendous, stained, twig teeth. 'We would have you know, that we could - if provoked - defend ourselves pretty well with our roots and branches. They can surely apply a good sting. But, of course, because of the way we were cultivated, we would rather show your

Grandma our respect.'

'That's right!' Mel replied boldly, folding his arms across his chest. 'You should show her respect. No one disrespects my Grandma and get away with it; especially in her house.'

'Oh really ... I will try to remember that!'

The composed Elm tree with broad trunk and greyish brown bark was much taller than the Birch tree and more tactful with his comments. Observing him cautiously, Mel could see what his Grandpa meant about the height of Elm trees, because he had to bend almost in half to prevent his head from going through the ceiling.

The bolder Birch tree in comparison had a slender trunk and a silky, silver-coated bark. Mel noted with curiosity, that small sections of his bark appeared to be strangely peeling off, but, with the exception of this, and his ridiculous leafy face, with piercing eyes, he too had an air of composure. Mel had a hunch however, that he could be ruffled.

'Come now,' said Birchard, 'Don't be upset. Despite how it seems we have no wish to scare you. We just want to be your friends, so let's start again. After all, your wish and imagination gave us the power to free our roots and roam. A lovely, liberating feeling I might add.'

Birchard stretched his branch arms across the width of the dining room and attempted what appeared to be a creaky, stiff yawn, leaving Mel astonishingly speechless.

'Tell me,' said Elmstead, in a rather leisurely, posh, commanding English accent. 'Why would a young boy like you want to talk to trees like us hmmm? Your friends will think you're absolutely barmy, would they not?'

Mel shrugged his shoulders. 'I don't know,' he said, seemingly more in control of his fear and temper. 'I suppose I was just curious. I think trees grow so strong and tall; much taller than humans, maybe if they could, they would reach for the sky.'

'Now that would definitely be an impossible task Mel.'

'Some trees have huge trunks that I can't even put my arms around,' Mel continued, stretching his arms wide to emphasise the point. 'And, some have beautiful blossoms and fruits. Grandma had a pear and apple blossom tree in the garden of her old house. I wish I could seen them.'

'Why couldn't you?' asked Elmstead.

'Because I wasn't born yet silly,' Mel replied cheekily.

'Oh excuse me, now why didn't I think of that?'

'I think trees are just great. I would love to climb to the top of a huge tree, sit in between the branches and eat the fruits'.

'Well that is a very simple wish Mel,' You might do that sooner than you think.'

'You seem to have a bit of an adventurous spirit. I was beginning to think that you lacked courage,' said Birchard.

'Me ... lack courage ... no way! I am very brave - ask my Grandparents,' Mel replied proudly with his arms on his hips.

His eyes suddenly lit up as he had a thought. 'Hey, have you guys heard of mango trees?'

'Yes!' both trees replied.

'Mangoes are Grandma and Grandpa's favourite fruit. I would really love to see a mango tree.'

'Well, why don't you make a wish, we'll take you to see some,' said Elmstead.

'What! You mean you can ... you can ...'

'Yes!' replied Elmstead.

'But how?' Mel squeaked, 'that's impossible!'

'Go on then, make your wish we're not bluffing! Nothing is impossible when you know how.'

Although Mel doubted their proclaimed magical powers and sanity, he was willing to test them. The thought of an adventure was just too good an opportunity to miss. He closed his eyes to think of the words to make the wish, when Grandma Cee's voice, interrupted his thoughts.

'Mel, who are you talking to down there?' she asked. Mel gasped, but the trees seemed totally, unruffled by the intrusion. He realised without a doubt that he would be in serious trouble if she saw the wreckage and, most of all, two crazy looking tree creatures seated around her dining table.

Her heavy footsteps descended rapidly down the stairs and Mel knew that he definitely had to stop her ... right now! He rushed through the dining room door; closed it quickly and displayed the cute, dimpled smile that she loved as he said, 'I was only talking to myself Grandma.'

'But I heard voices. Who is in there?' she demanded.

'No one Grandma, it's just me and my toys.'

Before Mel could say another word, she pushed passed him and swung open the door. Mel nearly fainted at the thought of what could happen next.

He then froze when he heard her bewildered voice say, 'Oh dear! There is no one here, but I could have sworn I heard loud voices.'

Grandma Cee climbed the stairs to return to the vacuuming, leaving Mel speechless. He couldn't figure out what had just happened. How could she have missed them; they were huge and, what about the mess!

Once again, he just had to see for himself. Listening in at the door - it was dead quiet. He pushed the door slightly, then wider to get a full view and what he saw left him feeling, absolutely shocked.

Everything had magically returned to normal. The smashed patio door was now intact; trails of mud disappeared from the floor and, most puzzling of all, there were no trees with silly faces seated around the table - they had completely vanished.

Mel slumped to the floor in utter confusion. 'Oh my god, what's happening here? Was I just talking to two crazy looking trees, or just imagining things?'

Not able to find answers to his questions, he rose from the floor with a sudden surge of determination; a bit like when he threw a tantrum, swung open the patio door and rushed into the garden. Everything was very still, no creaking noise, rain, or sound of thunder.

He looked over the garden fence and to his surprise there they were, standing tall with glistening leaves. No silly faces, weird eyes, or twig fingers; just two normal trees, rooted to the ground just like his lovely Biology Teacher described.

Mel shook his head in disbelief. 'Nah ... this isn't happening! Someone or something is playing tricks on me; trying to make me look stupid or something.'

He stared quietly at the trees before uttering a sigh. He had no evidence of them materialising and wasn't sure if he would want to encounter them again, if by some chance he could wish them back to life. Walking away with his head hung low, he thought to himself, *there is no such thing as magical trees. Who have ever heard of such nonsense?* He jumped as a sound unexpectedly escaped from his lips that said, *'You have!'*

On his way back to the house, his eyes suddenly lit up 'My cousin Mikal will be here tomorrow,' he muttered quietly. *He's really fun to hang around with; well ... fun, when he's not trying to boss me round,* he thought. *Playing PS4 games will be a whole lot better than talking to silly trees.*

He arrived at the patio door grinning from ear to ear and turned to have one last look at the trees before reaching for the handle. He pulled it open and was about to step inside when he heard a voice in the wind. His heart skipped a beat, and a strange tingling sensation came over him, forcing him to stop and listen. The top of his head unbelievably started to feel like it was swelling several inches in the air.

'See you tomorrow at the magic hour Mel,' the voice said. Startled, he turned swiftly, looking here and there; fist clenched, ready to defend himself if need be, but there wasn't a soul to be seen, least of all a talking tree.

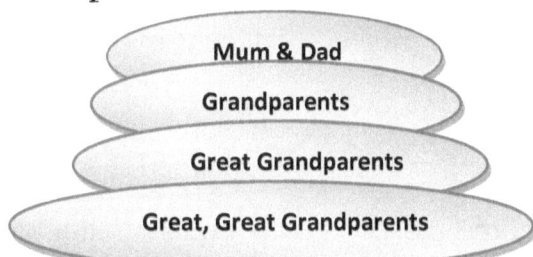

Mel woke up bright and early the next morning, feeling excited about seeing his cousin Mikal. They were spending the summer with their Grandparents' in Aylesbury, who simply adored them.

Tumbling out of bed, he drew the curtains. The sight of the squirrels scurrying up the ash tree and the sound of the birds brought a smile to his face, whilst the sun in the clear, blue sky made him feel alive and rearing to go.

His eyes drifted to the trees swaying in the morning breeze and a lump rose in his throat as memories of their encounter came flooding back. Deep down, he had an uncanny feeling that the memories he had been trying so hard to suppress were real. 'Maybe I was imagining things or, perhaps I was just halluci ... hallucinating. Trees can't talk or walk. It's just not normal,' he told himself firmly.

Mikal arrived with his dad Andre on time for breakfast with his thick black hair framing his brown, face. Their

Grandparents thought his beautiful brown eyes always portrayed an inquisitive, intelligent mind that was probably too advanced for a twelve year old.

Over breakfast, everyone chatted happily except Mel, who for some reason, could not stop thinking about the trees and fantasising about a flying trip, which he knew his Grandparents would not approve of.

Out of curiosity, he wondered if they did things at a younger age that their parents did not approve, and plucked up the courage to ask. 'No I didn't!' Grandpa Dee replied and diverted his attention to his newspaper.

'Me neither,' said Grandma Cee, concealing a tell-tale smile. 'If they were alive, my great grandparents would confirm this.'

'You knew your great grandparents?' asked Mel.

'Yes, they are my ancestors!'

'Ancestors ... what do you mean?'

'It's just the long line of family members - parents, Grandparents, great grandparents etc. that are on both sides of a person's family.'

'And, this line could stretch way back to when life began in Africa. But hey!' said Grandpa Dee casually, 'that's something for you boys to think about later.'

'Well, I read somewhere that Grandpa Dee's Mum was a linear descendant -whatever that means - of the African King Salmon Faye,' said Aunty Kede.'

'We have a real king for an ancestor!' said Mikal. 'Wow!

'Can you tell us about Great Grandpa Harold?' said Mel.

'He was great too,' said Grandma Cee. 'He made the finest suits in Jamaica, not even tailors in London's Savile Row could compete. As a preacher he was amongst the best; he even performed a miracle in his outdoor sermon, when he prayed for the rain to stop.'

'He prayed for the rain to stop... are you kidding?'

'No, your Great Grandma Millicent said after he did, it rained everywhere except where he preached.'

'Oh that's a miracle alright! Talk about Amazing Grace eh Cee - if you ask me that's definitely something to sing about!'

❧Chapter 4: Wishes & the Universe❧

*A*fter breakfast, Mel and Mikal decided to go for a ride on the garden swing. 'Come on Mikal push me higher,' said Mel. His legs swung high above the ground, passing very close to the trees he had doubts about the day before.

As he swung with the warmth of the sun and breeze swirling on his face, he felt as free as a bird; a sensation he wished he could enjoy forever. Some minutes passed, before a rustling sound in the wind almost made him topple off the swing in mid-air. *Huh! What was that?* He thought.

He balanced himself on the swing that he had stopped in mid-flow to listen. 'See you at the magic hour Mel. Your wish will definitely be granted then,' a voice said.

Mel gulped. 'Did you hear that?'

'Heard what Mel?'

'That sound -. that voice in the wind.'

'You're just imagining things like you always do. Come on, let's jump over the garden fence and climb those trees.'

'No ... I don't want to climb those trees.'

'Why not?'

'I just don't want to.'

'Ok suit yourself. I'm going to climb the Ash tree at the bottom of the garden.'

With Mikal out of the way, Mel was left alone to ponder on his thoughts. *Oh man, how could I even think that I was talking to trees -my friends would laugh in my face! Ha!*

He continued swaying thoughtfully to the creaking rhythm of the old swing, until he glanced at his new watch. It was almost lunchtime. Thinking of lunch made his taste buds come alive; he could almost taste the lovely aroma, until something interrupted his delicious thought. His mind drifted to that previous creaking sound.

'Nah, it can't be! I was only imagining things,' he tried to convince himself. He steadied the swing to listen closely. 'Shush!' he said, addressing the swing as if it were a life form.

There was that sound again, coming from the ground; startling him just like before; except this time, it grew unbearably louder, expanding all around him, penetrating his thoughts - he was definitely not dreaming now.

He jumped off the swing and as he landed, a tremor in the ground made him stumble. A spontaneous shriek unexpectedly came from his mouth and he clasped his hands over it, to prevent any further sounds from escaping.

Then he heard it - that deep Darth Vader-Optimus Prime voice he recalled from the day before. Mel covered his eyes, fearing what he might see or, most importantly, have to acknowledge. 'Hello Mel, remember us ... your tree buddies? Good to see you again!'

Mel peeked through his fingers and saw the mischievous smiling faces of Birchard and Elmstead peering back at him. 'Go away! Leave me alone you don't exist!' he yelled, tightening the gaps between his fingers.

'Not until you make your wish,' said Birchard. He leant forward to face Mel. 'You know, we trees are quite familiar with this "leaving" thing, because we grow leaves ... in abundance! But, on a more serious note, we are here to grant and fulfil your wish.'

'What wish?' Mel replied cheekily, peeking through his fingers again.

'The one you were about to make yesterday. Don't you remember? To go and see a mango tree, have you forgotten, or are you just scared?'

'Scared ... don't be silly!' Mel removed his fingers from his eyes to prove the point and then shifted from one foot to the next.

'Glad to hear it! You humans normally fear the unknown, but you know who we are Mel, don't you?'

Mel straightened his shoulders and nodded, but deep down he was not so sure -especially as they had disappeared before.

'We are just plain trees - transformed simply into a magical manifestation of your imagination.'

At that point, Mel glanced in the direction of the garden fence and to his surprise; the fence was still intact. 'Hey... wait a minute! How did you manage to uproot yourselves and cross over into our garden without damaging the fence this time?' he asked.

'Well we learnt from yesterday's unintended devastation that we have to respect other people's property,' Birchard replied.

'If you must know,' said Elmstead, 'We had to use a lot of nature's instant magic to put things back to normal. You know... that "Abracadabra" stuff,' he said casually. 'From now on, we'll simply levitate over the fence and that's a promise.'

Mel looked puzzled. 'Levitate ... over the fence ... are you guys crazy?'

'Yes, I mean ... no!

We just use the energies from our thoughts and vibrations to do this.'

'Vibrations, you mean all that shaking and stuff?'

'Yes it's a natural thing Mel. Everything vibrates, even you.'

'Really! Maybe I should check my pulse!'

'Yeah right! Let's just get back to the wish.'

'You two can't grant me a wish - you're just plain trees. You said that yourself.'

'Ah yes ... but you forgot the magic word Mel. We're magic trees; manifested because of your wish and ...'

'Yeah, yeah, I know!' Mel interrupted wearily. 'You have both manifested because of my wish and imagination ...right? So tell me ... how do you actually grant wishes?'

Elmstead leant clumsily forward and cleared his leafy throat. 'This is a bit hard to understand Mel but it's to do with our thoughts and the universe.'

'Thoughts and the universe - what do you mean? And what does the universe have to do with wishes? This wishing" thingy is really confusing.'

'Confusing! Not really ... it's basically about visualising what you want to achieve.'

'Ok! So I am thinking about getting a top grade for my Maths test; now what?'

'Well, "action follows thought" as they say. So, just add some positive thinking. Tell yourself that you can achieve it instead of the opposite. Then, focus and picture yourself gaining the grade and, don't forget to put in the hard work. All of this, plus the energies from your thoughts going out into the universe, can make it happen. Do you get it now?'

'I think so,' Mel replied. 'I have to think, focus and work hard; otherwise I won't get my wish.'

*A*gainst all odds, Mel finally decided to make the wish. 'Great! All you have to do now is make a wish for where you want to go and leave the rest to us,' said Birchard. 'We'll fly you there before you know it.'

'That sounds so ridiculous. I will look like an idiot flying in the air with you guys. I thought you had something better up your sleeve?'

'You won't look silly - you'll be wearing an invisible cape.'

'An invisible cape …can we go now please!'

'Certainly! Where to ... Africa, the Caribbean or India?'

'Mel, how about The Gambia .... Grandpa Dee's country?'

'Good choice ... there are many mango trees there. Do you speak Wolof, Jolof or Mandinka?'

Mel looked puzzled. 'No ... I only speak English!'

'That's ok - we speak many languages, depending on where our "roots" are. Hahaha! Did you get it?'

'Get what?' Mel asked blankly. He found Birchard's sense of humour a bit dry.

'Depending on where our roots ...' Birchard paused, hoping that Mel would catch on. 'Never mind - it's gone right over your head - whoosh!'

'Come on now Mel, just focus on where you want to get to and make the wish,' said Elmstead.

Mel closed his eyes. 'Ok, here goes! I wish that ...Wait!'

'Oh, what is it now?'

'Can I take my cousin Mikal? He's climbing the Ash tree at the bottom of the garden.'

'Mel we weren't thinking of taking additional passengers. After all, it was you who made the wish.'

'He'll be good I promise. Please, please, please say yes.'

'Alright!' said Birchard. 'Go and fetch him quickly, we must leave at the magic hour.'

Mel ran towards the Ash tree. He could hardly contain himself. 'Mikal come quickly,' he yelled. 'I am going on a journey; I have to make a wish!'

Mikal descended from the Ash tree, wondering what Mel

was talking about … it didn't make any sense!

'I want to take you on a flying trip.'

'What! Have you gone crazy? All that swinging in the air must have made the blood rush to your head.'

Mikal stepped out from behind the tree and froze when he saw the magic trees that had now made themselves visible to him too.

'Huh! What the heck!'

'Ah! No swearing allowed young man,' said Birchard. He paused briefly to brush his leafy shoulders with his twigged fingers; leaving Mikal feeling astonished. Then, he cleared his throat, smiled and welcomed him in his deep, Darth Vader Optimus Prime tone. 'Hi there, my name is Birchard, and this is my close friend Elmstead.'

'How do you do?' they both said, extending their branch arms for a handshake like they previously did to Mel. 'It's very nice to meet you!'

'Get away from me you freaks!' Mikal yelled, backing away quickly out of their reach

'Don't worry, they won't hurt you. They're my friends.'

'Friends, what made you think that Mel? These weird looking creatures aren't your friends.'

'Shush Mikal! Hold my hand. I need to make a wish. I want to go see a mango tree.'

'A mango tree! What's going on? Hold on, where did you meet these freaky things that have filled your head with such nonsense?'

'Alright if you must know Mikal; in our Grandparents' dining room yesterday. They really scared me when they spoke and tried to act like humans.'

'Oh really?' said Birchard glancing at Elmstead, you thought we were acting? Hmmm ... I quite fancy myself as a bit of a Thespian.'

'A Thespian?'

'An actor silly ... you know ... Shakespeare stuff. Birchard gestured with open arms, 'To be or not to be that is the question ..." What do you think?'

Mel looked at him blankly without acknowledging his question or performance, but Mikal's face lit up as he thought of something. 'So ... let me guess. Did someone or, something accidentally or deliberately, sprinkle you both, with magic dust or, some sort of spell for you to manifest as freaks or wannabe actors?'

'Yeah ... that's about right,' said Birchard. 'Except that it was your cousin here, who sprinkled the magic dust, or spell using his vivid imagination. There is a lot to be said for the power of thought.'

'Why don't you; if you so wish, give us a proper greeting using that hidden acting talent of yours that you got from your dad Andre. Or, alternatively,' Elmstead teased, 'you could watch us do a reality freak show.'

'How did you know about my dad and my acting talent?' 'I'm telepathic ... haven't you guessed?' Now, what will it be, you acting a scene, or us doing a freak show to fulfil your perception of what you think we are? Perhaps you'd like to be freaked out!'

'Come on Mikal, you started this, so let's just get it over with. I have an idea. Why don't we greet them as if we were a noble African king and prince and welcome them to our land. You can be the king - I don't mind.'

The magic trees looked on amused, whilst Mel and Mikal got into character and pretended to be dressed in the finest colourful, royal African gowns. Together, they flicked their imaginary gowns over their shoulders, bowed graciously and greeted them simultaneously. 'Welcome to our territory oh noble tree kings we are very honoured to meet you.'

Birchard responded in a voice that sounded very much like the actor James Earl Jones; or, was it Darth Vader! 'Thank you my noble King and Prince, we are delightfully, honoured to meet you too.'

Elmstead joined in, 'A king and prince shall we say that's endowed with powers to create magical creatures, using such vivid imagination.'

Mel stepped forward and bowed, 'Thank you oh noble ones for such honorary compliments.'

Mikal bowed again, 'Your Majesties, we would like to welcome you both by offering you gifts.' He extended his arm in the direction of the invisible gifts, 'Please choose from amongst our splendid treasures -gold, silver or diamonds.'

Both Trees bowed stiffly as Elmstead responded, 'Thank you oh noble ones. 'We're delighted to accept your splendid gifts that will be treasured for many moons to come.'

'I think this calls for a toast,' said Birchard. 'Let's raise our glasses to our noble friends.'

Jointly they raised their imaginary glasses, supposedly full of apple juice -Mel's favourite - and said 'Cheers to a lasting friendship great ones,' and followed this with a final bow.

The magic trees applauded and said, 'Bravo! Bravo! Bravo!' 'I think we could all make it to the Albert Hall!'

Mikal suddenly felt a draught on his rear end and realised that as he bowed, his shorts had embarrassingly slipped below his bum, exposing his underwear. *How gross!*

Elmstead glanced at him quizzically. 'Is that the new fashion?' he asked.

Mikal pulled up his shorts and to their amusement replied, 'No, it's just a "hang em" loose trend. Hahaha!'

'Now, back to the wish my nobles,' said Birchard. 'Mel for the last time please, makes your wish!'

Mikal clutched Mel's hand with some concern as he made his wish, and watched with curiosity as a ray of sunlight penetrated the ground and lingered for a few seconds. *Magical sunrays,* he thought.

With a swish of their branch arms, the trees miraculously draped the boys in a leaf coloured invisible cape like super heroes. Strong root belts, cleverly protruding from their branches, secured them into their sturdy branch seats and they were now ready to depart.

The boys suddenly felt a twinge of guilt about leaving without informing their grandparents.

'They won't suspect a thing said Elmstead. We'll return at exactly the same time we've left - 12:00pm - the magic hour, and you will be protected throughout.' This was reassuring to hear, but the boys knew their grandparents would never have consented to them going on this magical, flying journey.

'We will be invisible to all, except ourselves, and will be able to see, touch and hear everything around us,' said Elmstead.

'We will be invisible, just like the invisible man? That's Awesome!' said Mikal.

*E*lmstead started the countdown, '9, 8, 7, 6, 5, 4, 3, 2, 1. Houston, we have lift-off!'

Mel and Mikal screamed with excitement as the trees went up into the warm summer skies with a great whoosh. Higher and higher they flew, until their whole neighbourhood was hardly visible.

Birds that would normally look like a speck from the ground flew by with widespread wings, and fleeting clouds of all shapes, dotted the skies under the dazzling sun.

Mel thought they looked like floating, fluffy pillows and imagined drifting on an ocean made entirely of clouds. 'Ah this is the life!' he said. However, his fantasy ended with a puff when quite abruptly, they stopped in mid-air and he jerked back to reality.

'We're going to fall!' he yelled.

'Just hold on,' said Birchard, 'you're going to have the

journey of your life!'

What happened next was unimaginable. There was a flash of blinding light, which lingered in mid-air-and then transformed into an oval-shaped entity.

Breathtaking, sparkling blue shades that seemed to flicker to a rhythm they could not hear, streamed from its interior. Dazzled by its appearance, the boys were too stunned to speak. They clung on tight and waited anxiously for what would take place next.

Both trees began to spin very slowly at first, and then faster and faster in mid-air, leaves rustling and roots swirling until they were hardly visible to the naked eye. The boys felt like they were sitting on an uncontrollable spinning top that made their heads swirl with every rotation.

The trees then spun into the seamless, dazzling object that miraculously expanded to accommodate their great height, before taking off at a steady glide.

Inside the air was surprisingly cool and much bigger than how it appeared externally. Its entire length was beyond what the eyes could see. Dazzling, blue lights shone from every visible corner of the object that was unbelievably, operated by some invisible force.

At first, it felt like they were floating through the air, similar to the clouds. Then, without warning, the object zoomed through the air at great speed, just like the Star Ship Enterprise, daring to go where no one had ventured before.

In what seemed like seconds, they came to a standstill and the dazzling interior mysteriously changed shape. The boys and the magic trees descended to the ground; feeling as if they had slid through a long, gleaming tunnel that unexplainably disappeared out of view as soon as they landed.

'That was awesome ... fantastic! What sort of tunnel thingy was that?' the boys asked.

The trees displayed their familiar mischievous grin as Birchard responded. 'A tunnel, what tunnel? That, my noble friends, is a "state of the art" vortex.'

'A state of the art what?' they both shrieked.

$\mathcal{D}$isorientated and a bit stunned from their incredible flight, the boys peered through the branches of the magic trees. 'Where are we?' they asked.

'In Africa - The Gambia just like you wished. This is where life began for you humans - that's cool isn't it?'

'Actually Birchard, it's rather overheated if you ask me. I am just too accustomed to the English weather.'

'Well that's not surprising Elmstead, after all you are an English Elm. Try adjusting your heating mechanism.'

'Ok ...point taken. Are you guys ready to explore? With our inbuilt compass for direction and I as your world historian, we'll easily find our way around!'

'We could take them on a "wild" trip first. The Abuko Nature Reserve is a great place to start,' said Birchard.

Before they knew it, Mel and Mikal were back in the branches of the trees, feeling very excited and soon spotted the Reserve in the distance, surrounded by many trees and stretching for more than 250 acres. From above, the whole scenery resembled a forest; something the boys had never seen before. A wooden bridge extended through the Reserve, and an interesting nature trail led to a thick growth of vegetation that Elmstead referred to as a thicket.

Covered with the trees' mosquito, repellent juice and their invisible capes, Mel and Mikal set about exploring the amazing Reserve as soon as they landed. The sound of buzzing insects immediately filled their ears, whilst the smell of dried grass and other unidentified scents filled their nostrils. Never before had they seen so many colourful birds and animals all in one place.

Some of the animals roamed free and some were locked in cages. 'Birchard are they injured?' Mel asked.

'I don't think so Mel. They're probably locked up for public safety.'

Mel could not ignore the caged animals. He thought they should all be free to roam, so when Birchard went to join the others he decided to take action. A key invitingly stuck out of the lock from one of the cages. Unnoticed, Mel crept up to the cage and without fully, paying attention to the animals inside, unlocked it. He hid behind a bush as the animals wandered out and then strolled off to join the others; smiling as he thought of his good deed for the day.

The mysterious thicket near the nature trail looked like an interesting place to visit. Peering through from the edge, both boys wondered what could possibly lay hidden behind such a mysterious, thick overgrowth of shrubs and trees. They were about to venture in when Mel had second thoughts.

'Nah! I am not going in there -it's too thick. We'd have to fight our way through those shrubs.'

'Yeah right! Mel you're just worried that something might jump out and scare you.'

'Who said I'm worried. I'm not scared of anything in there or out here,' Mel bragged.

As he said that, they heard a sharp cracking sound behind them. It sounded like someone or something had just stepped on a twig. Mel jumped, let out an uncontrollable shriek, and embarrassingly turned around to see a mischievous monkey staring back at him.

'Shoo! Get out of my way,' he yelled.

'Hahaha! Thought you weren't scared of anything in there, or, out here,' teased Mikal.

On the Reserve, some of the animals found shelter from the hot sun beneath shady trees, or tried to cool themselves by the stream, which is where Mikal spotted the African crocodile. Its beady eyes gave him the creeps and its thick skin looked like a thousand bumps had embedded themselves in the grooves.

The crocodile had short legs and sharp looking teeth, inside the longest mouth Mikal had ever seen; and Elmstead warned him to steer clear. Although the crocodile looked dangerous, Mikal felt that he had nothing to fear. Compared to the pre-historic dinosaurs this crocodile is relatively harmless, he thought.

'Luckily a meteorite shower wiped out the dinosaurs millions of years ago, if not, I dread to think what would have happened to humans and the creatures they preyed on,' said Elmstead.

'And what about you trees?' replied Mikal. 'Some of the dinosaurs as you know were herbivores, so I should think life would have been just as difficult for you all.'

Mikal got distracted gazing at the dozing, sunbathing crocodile; wondering what it would be like if, it really got going. He discreetly threw a stone at it, and felt amused when it twitched, so he threw another and another, to provoke it further.

It wasn't long before the disturbance agitated the crocodile. It made an unexpected dash, towards a very surprised Mikal, who quickly leapt out of the way, escaping its huge jaws. However, the irate crocodile did not give up. It made another quick dash for Mikal as he tried to run off.

Mikal slipped and fell and to his horror, realised that this time, the crocodile had caught the left foot of his trainers in its mouth. He turned on his back and yanked the trainer free just before the crocodile's mouth slammed shut, then realised that his long, untied lace was wedged between its teeth.

The clever crocodile started moving backwards and Mikal found himself being, slowly dragged along the gritty ground, by his trainer lace towards its mouth. He twisted; turned and tugged on the lace several times to jerk it free, but it was stuck! Mikal called out for help and thought it went unheard.

From the corner of his eye, he was shocked to see another crocodile creeping up on the scene, looking just as fierce as the first. Then the battle began to see which one could get to him first. The second crocodile attacked the first one from behind and Mikal grabbed hold of a nearby tree as these huge crocs tossed and turned.

With the lace stuck in the crocodile's mouth, Mikal's leg was pulled in all directions and he became concerned about his safety, when he realised his grip on the tree was gradually loosening. When the first crocodile managed to throw off the second crocodile from its back, Mikal lost his grip on the tree and fell. The crocodile dragged him off once again, until his foot was only inches away from its jaws, with the lace wedged between its sharp teeth.

The crocodile opened its great jaws that looking like it was ready for a bite and at that moment, Mikal had to think of a way to save himself. He grabbed a piece of broken branch that had fallen off the tree he had clung to, and quickly pulled himself up as if he was doing a sit-up exercise.

Diving forward, he jammed the branch firmly inside his mouth to form a wedge. The infuriated crocodile shook its head from side to side, trying to dislodge the wedged branch, but it held firm. Mikal was more alarmed when the second crocodile was moving towards him again, and he couldn't find anything more to use, to defend himself.

Every-thing that he could possibly use was out of reach. He shouted for help hoping that someone would come to his rescue. Then he had another idea. He sprung up again, much quicker than before, stretched himself fully to reach inside the crocodile's mouth, and with a strong, swiftly tug on the lace managed to wrench it free.

The crocodile in its tail-lashing fury, pressed his jaws firmly against the jammed wedge, and this time it snapped with a cracking sound, moments after Mikal withdrew his hand. With no time to lose, he picked himself up and limped off with the trainer hanging off his heel.

Glancing back, he could see that both crocodiles were now in hot chase and he ran towards a path leading to a dead end. Realising he was cornered; he had no choice but to turn, and face them. They were steadily creeping up on him and, at the same time, signalling to each other with a flick of their jaws to back off their prey. Mikal had nowhere to run without at first attempting to jump over both crocodiles, which was an action he dreaded - but help was at hand.

Suddenly he heard what sounded like an aeroplane and

saw Birchard zooming down on the crocodiles. He grabbed the tail of the second one and threw it aside. It landed on its back; flipped over onto its stomach and slithered off. The first crocodile's huge tail swished frantically from side to side when Birchard jumped on its back, but he wrestled with it firmly, until he eventually pushed it off the path and cleared the way for Mikal to get through.

Mikal didn't hesitate; without looking back, he ran as fast as he could, away from the crocodile and its huge, snapping jaws. He was still actually shaking from the crocodile encounter, when Birchard caught up with him.

'That was a lucky escape,' said Birchard. 'Why did you disturb the crocodile that was snoozing so peacefully? I told you to stay clear of it. Maybe I need to link you up with Crocodile Dundee.'

Mikal didn't say a word throughout the telling off, because Birchard's Dart Vader-Optimus Prime voice was so penetrating, and he really couldn't think of an excuse for his behaviour. However, it wasn't long before he recovered from this escapade and rushed off with Mel to see what else they could find interesting to explore.

There was so much more to see on the nature reserve. African Crown Cranes rummaged through the grass with brightly coloured Mohican style crowns, that reminded the boys of the seventies punk fashion.

An interesting herd of animals were at the stream, some with horns protruding from the top of their heads or spots that Mel wanted to stroke. 'You will do no such thing!' said Elmstead. 'Those are bushbucks, a type of antelope that can be very dangerous if attacked.'

Ah! So that is what's in the thicket - they aren't scary at all.

Mel was very mistaken as he soon found out. Standing by the stream, he peered in the distance against the glare of the sun, at a shadowy figure in the thicket.

As he could not make it out, he turned his attention to the rest of the surroundings and noted that a troop of Baboons had for some reason, climbed to the safety of the trees. They were pulling faces and making a strange,

"Wahoo" barking sound, as if they were sending a signal.

The bushbucks at the same time pricked up their ears as if sensing approaching danger and quite unexpectedly, started running in the opposite direction from the stream. As the boys looked on, the mysterious figure in the thicket revealed itself. A 5ft long, spotted leopard sprang out of the bushes, with its long tail trailing behind him.

In an instant, it started chasing the bushbucks that by now were running frantically towards them and the magic trees and the other animals instinctively scarpered out of their way.

Faster and faster the bushbucks ran, whilst the leopard, their main predator, was rapidly catching up, leaving the boys gasping at his speed.

'Get out of the way,' yelled Birchard. 'You'll get trampled.'

Mel and Mikal had almost made it to safety behind a large boulder, when the bushbucks stampede crashed past

them, kicking up a cloud of dust that sent them flying onto their backs. They had definitely had a lucky escape!

Scrambling to their feet, they continued watching the amazing chase. It was almost as if they were caught up in the middle of a 3D film with front row view. Meanwhile, the bushbucks continued to flee for their lives with the leopard swiftly catching up.

The leopard pounced on the back of a young bushbuck that immediately fell beneath it, pinning it down with its strong muscles. As the leopard aimed to sink its sharp teeth into the bushbuck, a siren suddenly echoed loudly throughout the nature reserve.

The startled leopard released its grip to look around, allowing the clever bushbuck to seize the opportunity to escape, and run off to catch up with the rest of his herd. However, the leopard was not about to let it get away that easily.

It quickly resumed the chase with long swift strides,

which gave it the edge to outrun the bushbucks. Then, just as it looked set to pounce a second time, there was that strange noise again; echoing through the resort in quick spurts louder than before.

The leopard paused, looking just as startled as before and to the boy's delight, the bushbuck grabbed a second chance to escape its jaws. Defeated, it watched as the herd of bushbucks disappeared into the distance and some minutes later, headed back towards the thicket, leaving the lucky bushbucks to live another day.

'Where did that sound come from Elmstead?'

'Well that was good timing Mikal. The rangers set off the siren, after discovering that the caged animals had escaped, and were concerned for the safety of the tourists. It seems someone had the bright idea to unlock their cage. It wouldn't by any chance be one of you guys, would it?'

Mikal glanced at Mel and for once remained quiet.

'Actually, I believe it was ...' Birchard paused to look at both boys sternly. 'Nah, don't worry, they just wouldn't be that stupid. Isn't that right Mel?'

❦Chapter 9: The Hyenas❧

$\mathcal{T}$he travelling party was about to take to the air after the bushbuck incident, when they noticed a pack of animals staring in their direction. At first Mikal wasn't sure what they were. When they walked, their slight bear-like build confused him a bit. *Were they bears or wolves?*

The spots on their tanned pelts reminded him of Dalmatians, who perhaps, he imagined, looked a lot friendlier.

'These hyenas can sense our presence?' said Birchard.

'Hyenas - so that's what they are!' said Mikal. 'But we're invisible ... aren't we? They shouldn't be able to see us.'

Suddenly, Mel realised that his good deed for the day, had come back to haunt him. He had discretely released these same animals from their cage earlier.

'Uh oh!' he cried out, but it was too late.

With their heads held low, the hyenas started making a peculiar whooping sound, which escalated into a low-pitched grunt. As this became more high-pitched, it sounded like a strange laugh. *How odd!*

Mel and Mikal quickly climbed into their branch seats, and to their amazement, the hyenas started moving slowly towards the trees and then in a frenzied run to attack.

Their ridiculous grunt and cackling laugh echoed through the air as they surrounded and attacked the trees, scratching, biting and painfully tearing off strips of their barks. *Ouch!*

The invisible magic trees fought back, lashing out with their branches and entwined roots but the fierce attack continued - they were outnumbered!

The Rangers and visitors stared at the strange sight, wondering what could be disturbing the animals that were attacking thin air. There was no one in sight!

Suddenly, a thin, white mist with a strange scent began to form in the air. It filtered down like a vapour and within minutes, surrounded the hyenas. The overpowering scent penetrated their nostrils when they sniffed the air, and before long they started rolling on the ground as if they were intoxicated.

The boys thought the hyenas had taken ill from the

scent, but then noticed that as they rolled about on the ground with paws in the air, their strange cackling laugh was bizarrely twice as loud. They had never seen animals behave like this. Anyone looking on would believe the hyenas were having a whale of a laugh, but who was telling the jokes?

'What happen to them?' the boys asked as they were taking off in the branches of their injured magic trees.

'Oh nothing too drastic,' replied Elmstead. 'They just inhaled a bit of relaxing, scented gas that turned their viciousness into a bit of harmless laughter.'

'Wait a minute,' said Mikal. 'You guys gave them Laughing Gas? Hahaha, that's so sick!'

∽Chapter 10: Birds & Green Mamba∾

They soared through the air observing the beautiful scenery with colourful homes and busy streets; unnoticed by those beneath scurrying about their daily business. There were many beautiful birds with squawking sounds welcoming the party of flying travellers.

'Africa is an amazing place,' said Mel. 'Even the birds are friendly.' Mel suddenly realised that he had spoken too soon, when he let out a piercing scream. 'A snake! Birchard ... Elmstead, help!'

Birchard peered through his branches and saw a long, green snake with an orange tail, slightly camouflaged against the leaves, wriggling his way up the branch towards Mel. 'A Green Mamba Snake!' he said surprisingly.

'It must have crept on at the nature reserve. Hold on tight Mel.'

The slithering snake, with its darting tongue tasting the air, crept up Birchard's trunk, heading straight for the branch where Mel sat. Birchard flicked a twisted root at the snake a few times. It flinched and hissed with every lash, as it continued on its creepy path, wriggling its way up the branch whilst exposing its inner white jaws and fangs. Mel, by now could almost imagine its cold flittering tongue connecting with his skin.

It seemed like there was no hope of disengaging this creepy predator from the branch, but the magic trees in a joint effort were not about to be defeated. With roots poised, they took aim. The whooshing sound of their double lashing roots, echoed through the air when it struck the snake's head in an attempt to dislodge it.

Unbelievably, its coiled tail finally loosened its grip. It somersaulted through the air, hissing continuously until it landed on the ground, several feet below with a thud that dispersed a large stream of dust in the midday air. They all remained silent - no one dared to look to see if it was still alive, but its days were certainly over.

Mel could not help sobbing whilst Birchard used a leafy tissue to wipe way his tears - after all, he had just had a very close encounter with a very creepy reptile.

'It's alright now,' he said. 'We'll have to be more

selective about whom we give a ride to in future, because we only want agreeable folks travelling with us ... right!'

'Right!' Mel replied, smiling through his tears.

As the flight through the Gambian skies continued with the sun on their backs, thoughts of the slithering close encounter were all too soon forgotten - replaced instead, by exciting thoughts of their next landing.

❧Chapter 11: The Deserted School House❧

Banjul was once again on the horizon. The trees swooped to the ground with the boys in their branches, as the breeze filled their T-shirts like a hot air balloon. 'Whoopee, this is fun! You should thank me for bringing you along to this sunny Motherland Mikal.'

'Well thanks a lot Mel. Does anyone have a fan?'

Elmstead gave the boys a leafy hat to protect their heads from the sun that would definitely spoil their "street cred" back home. Sweat dripped down their slightly, flushed brown cheeks and, to make matters worse, the dusty ground stained their trainers with a reddish hue.

Fussy Mel was not impressed. The trees on the other hand, looked as cool as a cucumber - their cooling mechanism was definitely intact! The scene was bursting with a multitude of colours, modern and colonial buildings. Even the traditional garments worn by Gambians seemed to reflect the hot, sunny climate.

'I really like this place,' said Elmstead. 'Maybe I'll visit it again on a solo trip ... in spirit mind you!'

'Oh come off it, trees don't have a spirit.'

'Yes, we do Mel. We call it the "KA" like your ancestors, those great Pharaohs in Ancient Egypt.'

'The KA!' Mel repeated. 'That sounds kinda cool, but I'm gonna ask Grandpa Dee about those Pharaohs!'

Venturing onto the main road, they could hear the laughter and happy chatter of the children playing games above the bustling sound of the city. Turning into a lane, Mel saw an old school building with a flat roof, spreading across its width. From a distance, the windows peeked out from beneath the roof like guarding eyes.

The hinges on the wooden gate were squeaking in tune with the gentle river breeze and the playground shimmered under the hot sun. Mel sensed a familiarity with this old, yet inviting school building. It was almost as if he had been a pupil there. He decided then that, he had to explore it.

Without notice, he rushed off through the squeaky, school gates; pushed open the doors to the deserted building and entered cautiously. The eerie silence and echo of his footsteps, almost made him run back to the company of the Trees, but trying to be brave as usual, he continued.

Mel curiously peered through the doors of the classrooms on either side of the corridor that were dim in the absence of the sunlight. A few student lockers lined the corridor walls, and one of the doors was invitingly ajar.

He peaked into its vacant, dusty space and brushing the cobwebs aside, picked up the remains of a tattered newspaper from the bottom, with the title, *"The Point Newspaper, Banjul, Gambia."*

He skimmed through some of the headlines that caught his eye; *"Banjul teenager won the award for best sports student". "Comprehensive Senior Secondary School prepares students for programs leading to award".*

'Sounds cool, one day I'll be a "headliner" just like them.'

It dawned on him then that he sounded just like Grandpa Dee, who had always wanted to be a star. He picked up a tattered, discarded notebook and shook the dust from its pages. His hand brushed against something cold and clammy that immediately responded by emitting a croaking sound.

He quickly withdrew his hand, fell backwards and shrieked as a bumpy, toad leapt out in his path. It jumped across his chest with drooping legs brushing his face, then hopped to the end of the corridor; "ribbitting" all the way.

'I can't stand toads he said, they are so gross!'

Mel entered a few classrooms, looked around. Just as he was about to end his tour, for no particular reason, he decided to enter one last room that caught his attention - the classroom to the left!

Opening the creaking door, he walked in quietly, as if not to disturb a class in flow. Seated around a desk with arms folded, he imagined the room to be full of students, listening to his Great Grandma teaching a Science lesson.

He was so deeply engrossed in the scene that he mentally blocked out the cough from an unidentified source that echoed in the room. He heard it the second time, believing it to be a part of his imaginary scene, but when the sound reached his ear a third time, he realised it was real. He gulped and turned to see a tall, masculine bearded figure, wearing a khaki uniform, staring vacantly towards him, with one arm resting on the doorpost.

Mel's brow puckered into an anxious frown and remembering that he was invisible, bravely jumped up to sprint to the door; aiming to zip under the arms of the bearded man, as the desk and chair toppled behind him.

Then the man spoke, or rather bellowed in a startling voice that was much less frightening than Birchard's. 'What on earth is that?' he said, 'Come on show yourself!'

He lunged forward; eyes searching frantically for the unseen stranger, ready to grab whatever came his way, but instead, he slammed into Mel and they both tumbled onto the floor. Mel picked himself up and bolted as fast as he could through the door; glancing behind at intervals.

An image of Usain, his Jamaican sport hero sprung to mind, as he sprinted in trainers that hit the floor with a squeaky thud. His invisible cape slipped below his waist and he could hear the stranger's footsteps pounding heavily behind him, Mel struggled to pull the cape, back onto his shoulders, but not before the stranger caught a glimpse of him becoming partly visible.

Convinced that it was a prank, the stranger's long, muscular arms kept clutching at Mel and as his torso faded back into invisibility, he continued the chase on pure instinct. Using every ounce of strength, Mel kept running at break neck speed through the corridor, which seemed much longer than when he had entered.

At one point, with his chaser inches away, he thought he might never make it to the entrance, but he kept up the pace, until finally, the sunlight hit his frantic face that was absolutely dripping with sweat. Exhausted, Mel ran towards Mikal and the now very stern looking magic trees.

He slumped, exhausted at their feet, and then turned to look at the stranger, who was leaning against the doorframe panting.

'Eh, what on god's earth was that ... the invisible man, or a mischievous spirit?' he said between breaths. 'Don't know why I took on this humdrum, caretaking job. With all my qualifications, I deserve much better than this!'

The travelling party continued their journey, after Mel got a telling off for trespassing. On the way, they saw a sign pointing to the Veterinary Centre, where they thought their Great Uncle Sanji worked.

As they approached the family home, situated near the Centre, they heard a female voice say, 'Jamos, I have just cleaned the house get those muddy shoes off.'

'Sorry Nyima - didn't mean to make a mess,' he replied.

Nyima's bright blue kaftan worn with matching head dress, puffed out with the hot breeze, as she called out to another young man in the yard. 'Sajaa are you still feeding those hens? Why don't you get your sister to help?'

Mel and Mikal looked at each other and felt excited - they had found their cousins!

'Seems like your uncle has hired a housekeeper Mel, is he rich?'

'Dunno Elmstead, you would have to ask him that. Can we get a drink? I haven't had one since we left home.'

'Me too,' said Birchard, licking his lips. 'I could do with some of our delicious glucose. By the way Mel, what exactly do you mean by "Dunno" is that short for I do not know?'

'Yes of course,' Mel replied. 'It's just the way young people like us say it sometimes. If you are going to hang around us Birchard, you need to get with the times!'

'Wow! Excuse me!' said Birchard.

'What about that glucose you were talking about, I think you trees are so weird!' Mikal commented.

'That's very true! Elmstead replied. After all Mikal, we are not you and you are not us, but we need each other to survive. You need our oxygen and we need your Carbon Dioxide.'

'Did you say Carbon Dioxide? I've just been learning about that in my Science class, but to be honest it's a bit boring.'

Elmstead touched Mikal's shoulders 'You know what, I have a feeling that from now on you're going to find Science subjects a lot more interesting.'

'Mel, why don't you and Mikal sneak into your uncle's kitchen and get a drink.'

'No way, we can't do that Birchard. We are not thieves!'

'Ok, maybe you should think about the dehydration option then!'

Without another word, the boys strolled off into their uncle's brightly painted yellow kitchen, and opened the fridge. Lots of delicious food and drinks were inside, including a lovely jug of lemonade that they could not resist - it looked and tasted so good.

They were about to pour out some more lemonade, after the second glass, when Mel noticed that the kitchen door had swung open. A woman dressed in a nurses uniform with hair swept neatly back under a cap, stood at the entrance.

She had watched dumbfounded as drinks from the fridge floated through the air; then poured out into tilted glasses by unseen hands, and amazingly drained of their contents into unseen mouths.

When Mel noticed her standing there watching in fear, he was so shocked, the glass of lemonade slipped out of his hands and crashed to the floor. The crash scared the woman even more, so she dropped her bag and ran out of the kitchen.

'Come quickly ... there is a ghost in the kitchen pouring

out my lemonade,' she stuttered to Nyima. 'Come and look!'

Nyima had a confused look on her face, because normally she was a very calm and dignified woman - not one to cause a scene.

'What are you talking about Mrs Ida?' She replied 'I cleaned the fridge this morning and made fresh lemonade; there were no ghost in the house. I think you are a bit tired, maybe you need to rest.'

'But I saw it with my own eyes Nyima - you must believe me!' she stressed. 'It broke my glass! I tell you what ... hurry... go and fetch my husband Sanji from the veterinary centre; he will sort this out.'

'Mel that's our great uncle's wife, Aunty Ida, we had better get out of here!'

Uncle Sanji was a rather serious looking professional Vet, with a good sense of humour that he only shared with a few people.

'I can't see anyone or anything here sipping our lemonade,' he said to his wife, who was attempting to explain what she had witnessed. 'It's all in your imagination.'

'Maybe our house is haunted?' she replied.

'Certainly not! But, if there are any ghosts or spirits hiding in this house,' he said jokingly, 'The priest is on standby, so trust me, they will be in for some serious exorcising.'

A bewildered Aunty Ida took her husband's advice to get some rest and went off to bed. Later when Nyima went to pour herself a drink from the fridge, she was rather puzzled to find that the lemonade jug; smeared with dirty fingerprints was almost drained.

'Eh! What happened to the lemonade?' she muttered. She searched the fridge for leakage, but there was no sign of this. Then to make things worse, she slipped on the lemonade spillage.

'Maybe Mrs Ida was right,' she said rubbing her bruised knee. 'There must be spirits around here, but they'd better get out of my way,' she mumbled, staggering out of the kitchen, 'Cos, I'm definitely not messing!'

❧Chapter 13: The Green Monkeys❧

The huge mango tree at the back of their uncle's house looked like a giant umbrella with branches spreading nearly a 100 feet.

'Now that's what I would call a very "shady" tree indeed,' Elmstead mischievously joked.

The boys couldn't wait to pick the tasty red tinged, ruby mangoes, but climbing this huge tree looked like a difficult task, much harder than climbing the Ash tree back home. 'Go ahead!' said Birchard. 'We'll be watching you.'

And so, the boys began the long climb. Inch by inch they scaled the tree trunk; firmly gripping each notch, until at last they seated themselves on a sturdy branch.

Lovely ripe mangoes hung in clusters from almost every branch and the boys picked a few and ate them "messy" style instead of diced. Delicious mango juice smeared their mouths and at that moment, sweets back home were no

comparison.

When it was time to attempt the long climb back, it proved to be much more difficult than climbing up. Pausing briefly against the tree trunk, Mikal felt a sudden jerk in the branch above. Initially he thought it was the wind, but felt concerned when it jerked a second and third time.

Looking up, Mikal glimpsed a pair of fiery eyes peering back at him from the branch above. He blinked; there were two pairs ...no ... four pairs!

'Mel, look to your left. There is something weird in the branches above your head.'

Mel hadn't noticed. He was busy concentrating on getting his footing right. 'Oh come on Mikal, stop messing around and let's get down before we fall.'

'No seriously Mel, there is something up there - take a look!'

Mel looked up to see four pairs of red eyes, attached to

four furry faces staring back at him. 'Oh my gosh ... monkeys! They can see us like the hyenas.'

The monkeys stood up in unison revealing their creamy, gold and greenish furry body with a yellow-tipped tail.

Quite unexpectedly, they began to make a chattering sound. To the boy's amazement, they vigorously shook the branches and dispatched a pile of mangoes on their heads that almost sent them flying.

The mangoes landed hard on their heads and shoulders and to make matters worse, the monkeys seemed to be mocking the boys with their chatter as they pelted them. Clinging to the tree with one arm they, protected themselves with the other, but the force of the mangoes eventually made them lose their grip.

As they fell, the monkeys jumped up and down on the branch, and their chatter seemed to change suddenly, to a sound like a victory cheer. The somersault in the air seemed like forever, before the Mel and Mikal landed on what felt like a leafy bush.

'Caught you!' said a familiar voice. 'Did you guys fancy a bit of bungee jumping?

'Bungee jumping! Did you see those monkeys? Those cheeky things pelted us with mangoes. They were trying to drive us out of the tree.' replied Mikal. Elmstead and Birchard broke out in laughter. 'Those mischievous green monkeys pelted you?' They laughed so much that their barks showed signs of cracking and the boys were literally fuming at this point

'By the way, how were the mangoes?' asked Elmstead. 'They're filled with vitamin C, E and more you know.'

'Hmmm, they were really delicious. Wish we didn't have to travel so far to eat them.'

'Who said you had to boys? They are in supermarkets and greengrocers back home, but trust me; those will never taste as nice as the ones you've just eaten.'

ᛥChapter 14: The Guard Dogsᛥ

After the pelting jokes, the boys and the magic trees made their way towards the gate, unaware of the danger ahead. As they drew nearer to the gate, they were startled by the sound of the alarm. Someone had switched it on! Unexpectedly, two ferocious dogs; the type anyone would want to avoid, raced towards them with glistening, tanned fur.

For a fleeting moment, Mikal thought of the picture of the ferocious dog on his neighbour's door, and the sign below it, "COME ON MAKE MY DAY". Then he noticed there was a similar sign on his uncle's gate. *Uh oh!*

'Get up in the branches now,' said Birchard. They can see us like the hyenas.' With knees buckling, the boys scrambled to safety, whilst the dogs charged towards the magic trees, barking like something from a horror movie.

The hyenas bit their barks, ripped their invisible leaves from their branches, and scattered them across the ground as they tried to fight them off. The boys could see Birchard and Elmstead wincing from the attack.

Nyima came rushing out, wondering why they were barking crazily in front of a vacant space. 'Come on now, shut up that racket!' she said firmly. 'What are you barking at you silly dogs? Can't you see that there is no one there?'

She grabbed their leash and with great effort, attempted to drag them back to the house, but one of the dogs pulled away and ran back towards the trees, snarling and growling louder than before. It suddenly tilted its leg and peed on Birchard's trunk, before Nyima could drag him off again.

Birchard was furious. 'Did you see that?' he said. 'He did his business on me. What am I ... a peeing post? I have never encountered such a cheeky, vicious canine.'

Birchard could not see the funny side of it. He was still fuming, when they both dressed their wounds with leaf juice and covered them with weird, trunk-coloured plasters. When they were finished, they made their way towards the gate again.

The dogs now shackled to their post, began barking

once more, but to Birchard this was the last straw. He had had, enough of the dogs' commotion. He pulled out a long twisted root and like a circus master in a ring, flicked it sharply at the dogs without hitting them.

It whizzed through the air, dipped past the top of their mouths and hit the ground; almost travelling faster than the speed of sound, which is 344 metres per second, in dry air. Then to everyone's surprise, a much deeper Darth Vader-Optimus Prime tone exploded in the air, ordering the huge dogs firmly to 'SIT!' The dogs whimpered and retreated obediently to sit by their tethered post.

'Wow! That was quite scary and impressive,' said Elmstead. 'I felt sorry for those poor dogs.'

'You felt sorry for them! They nearly tore us to bits; didn't you notice? I travelled all this way to be peed on and attacked by fierce canines, not once, but twice, in one day.'

Elmstead had a grin spreading right across his face as he said, 'Hey... smile, give us a twirl - you have just been framed by Candid Camera.'

'Candid Camera ... what's that?'

'Dunno Mel, things are getting weirder around here.'

Chapter 15: The Ancient Tree Clan

Their travels took them to a field with Mango Kent trees and also an unusual tree bearing mangoes that actually resembled papayas. 'That's strange' said Elmstead. 'It is a Mango Papaya tree from Senegal - must be a stray!'

The boys had a choice of climbing whichever tree they thought had the most delicious looking mangoes. They chose a Mango Kent tree, with mangoes hanging in a rich green and red colour. Looking almost majestic, if such a thing could be said about trees, it was swaying in the breeze right beside the Mango Papaya tree.

The trees instructed Mel and Mikal to pick mangoes only from the branch they were sitting on, but the adventurous Mikal spotted a mango hanging on a higher branch that he could not resist. He climbed further up the tree, leant forward to pluck it and almost had it in his grasp, when he heard a cracking sound - the branch had snapped!

Mikal quickly grabbed hold of another branch wrapped

his legs around it and hung on for dear life. Looking down, as he feared, the ground below was a long way off. The slender branch dipped, lower and lower under his weight, until it eventually snapped, and Mikal found himself falling with nothing to grab to prevent him hitting the ground.

Mel saw what had happened and acting quickly, positioned himself flat on the branch, to grab Mikal as he fell. He missed, but managed to grab hold of his T-shirt and gripped it tight. Mikal was swinging back and forth in the air and Mel could feel the strain in his arm and the branch.

He knew that pretty soon, they would both be heading for the ground. Seconds later, the strength in his arm gave way, and Mikal's T-shirt gradually slipped through his fingers. Mel reached out and tried to grab his T-shirt again, but missed and lost his balance. 'Mikal nooooo,' he cried out as they both fell towards the ground.

Then something strange happened. It felt like the majestic Mango Kent tree had suddenly sprouted two protruding branches that were wedged under the boys T-shirts; suspending them in the air. The branches grated the skin on their backs as they swung from left to right, but at least they had not fallen to the ground - well, not yet! Inevitably, a few seconds later, there was another loud, cracking sound and they landed on an outstretched, lower branch of the Mango Papaya tree nearby.

Holding on tight, they were swinging again, wondering how they were going to get down. Suddenly the whole branch gave way and unbelievably, they vanished in mid-air.

Mikal heard the branch snapped and had quickly pulled his legs up to his chest to somersault to the ground, but he couldn't. Mel didn't have time to think of that strategy, he fell and tumbled towards the ground just like Mikal.

They were both flipping continuously in the air and everything around them seemed to be in a whirl; they hardly had time to catch their breath. Then suddenly it stopped as quickly as it began, and something was holding them up. *Thank goodness!* They thought. *But, what had just happened?*

In the midst of all the confusion, Mikal heard a voice say, 'Well look what we've got here! They've dropped out of the sky right into my branches.'

They boys had fallen into craggy, leafy palms that were most uncomfortable. Looking up, a giant leafy face, with huge brown eyes stared down at them. 'Who are you?' the boys asked, trying hard to sound brave.

'That's what we would like to ask you,' said the voice behind the leafy face. You are a bizarre looking pair. So tell me who are you?'

'We look Bizarre ... seriously! If you must know, I'm Mikal and this is my cousin Mel.'

'Oh ... so you have just dropped into my branches with your family. Did you bring your mum too?'

'No we didn't. Why are we in your hands?'

'You both tumbled out of my branches into my hands Mikal. Just what were you doing there I would like to ask?'

'We fell out of a Mango Papaya tree.'

'A Mango Papaya tree did you say? Hmmm ... sounds like a distant relative, for sure!'

The leafy face belonged to a giant mango tree that was much taller than their magic trees and, most of the other trees in the area. It looked like they were in an orchard in a strange land, but how could this be? Moreover, come to think of it, where are their magic trees that were supposed to be looking after their safety?

'Please put us down now,' said Mikal, 'we need to get

back to Birchard and Elmstead.'

'Who?'

'Our magic trees - they will be looking for us.'

'Well actually ... we would all like to request the pleasure of your company at our Honour Conference. We would like you both to attend. If you participate we will let you get back to your guardians in ... sorry, where did you say you were from?

'We didn't,' replied the boys.

'Oh, so where should we send you back to?'

'Alright!' said Mikal. 'We were in The Gambia in 1962 but originally from England in 2012.'

'2012 ... does the world still exist then? I thought it was predicted to be a "gonner" by that time.'

'The world still exists then and we need to get back now.'

'I'm happy to do that later if you will participate in our Honour Conference.'

'Honour Conference ... what's that?'

'Well, have a look around. We all look "rooted" but in fact, once a year we travel from far and wide to honour our oldest member, who many, many years ago drifted to this very spot as a seed and sprouted. Being the only mango tree here for years, she genetically merged with the papaya.'

'How long ago was that?'

'The seed landed in 1562 Mikal, so you do the Maths; I'm afraid I'm no Mathematician, but she's here now in disguise.'

The boys looked puzzled. 'Yes that's right,' said the giant mango tree. 'This special tree is a "She". Your task is to identify her from amongst all these trees and, name her title.

The boys could not believe what they had just heard. 'Are you joking? How are we going to do that? There are so many of you and we don't even know where we are.'

'You don't know where you are Mikal? Have a look around – you are in The Gambia. Ok, I admit it's not modern 1962 - it's actually 1862 - but it's still recognisable.'

'1862! Oh my days, we'll never get back now!'

'Well so much for optimism Mel. Anyway, back to the task. Here's a clue to help you, 'Age *is but a number that circles me like a ring. The first number is just that ... it's simply what I am.*'

Mel and Mikal pondered on this and after doing the Maths, figured that this ancient tree must be at least 300 years old. To find her, they were going to have to search amongst the older looking trees and count their growth rings - the layers of wood growth under their bark.

'Uh oh! That won't work,' said Mel. 'My Biology Teacher said there is one growth ring for each year of a tree's life. The rings in the trunk is only visible when the tree is cut down, or if a sample is taken from it, using an Increment Borer. I am not sure what that is, but we definitely can't do either of these.'

'I've just had a thought Mel. If a tree has been growing for 300 years, piling on those growth rings, it would have a very wide trunk by now.'

'That's right Mikal. You're a life saver!'

With the aid of Kenja, a tall, majestic tree, with the friendliest, dark brown eyes amongst all the trees, Mel & Mikal picked out the trees with very wide trunks to question.

To get the answers that would help to solve the puzzle, they were aiming to use some historical information that Grandpa Dee had taught them. The first question, '*Who were the first Europeans to trade in The Gambia?*' whittled down the number of trees to nine hopefuls, who said 'The

Portuguese.'

This answer gave the boys some indication of their age. The others did not have a clue. As obviously, they were not even sprouted by the 1700s! The boys thought hard about the next question, divided into two parts; *'What are the "conduct" rules that you all have to abide by?'*

All nine hopefuls answered, 'To show loyalty, honour and respect to the Ancient Tree Clan at all times.'

The boys then asked all nine, the second part of the question. *'And what would you do if these rules were dishonoured, by any member?'*

The ancient trees looked at them and frowned, as if to say it's impossible - this could never happen - but Mel and Mikal pushed for an answer. Each of the nine ancient trees had a different answer. Some said, 'Break off all their branches and leave them bare to be scorned.' Others said 'Cast them out - banish them from the land forever - turn them into firewood. Or, Stick lumps on their trunks.'

The last one said, 'Dishonouring the rules would be a very sad thing indeed. However, I would avoid harsh measures, if the clan member were willing to repent and abide by the rules. Keeping the family together would be my priority.'

The boys whispered together and then called the giant tree over. 'We've solved the puzzle,' they announced.

'Oh really - let's hear it then!'

Mikal was the first to break it down. 'We believe the first part of the clue *"Age is but a number that circles me like a ring..."* means the age of this special tree can be determined by the growth rings under its bark. As it is not possible to cut the trees down to count their rings, we made an assessment by their trunk width.

There was suddenly a lot of murmuring amongst the trees, 'Huh ... they thought about cutting us down! That's not allowed - some humans have no respect for nature. Measuring our trunks is a much better idea.'

Now it was Mel's turn. 'We figured that the second part of the clue; *"the first number is just that ...it's simply what I am "* had to be about the honorary tree's title. Our Grandpa told us the Gambian word "Kilifa" means "Chief" someone with authority; a leader, or the number one in a community.

Mikal placed his hand on a huge mango tree, much taller than the giant tree. 'We believe this tree was the first one here and the longest living tree in the orchard. It is the tallest, with the widest trunk that only 300 hundred years of existence could have produced.'

'We also believe that this tree is who you all refer to as the mother tree - the "Number One"- the crowned "Kilifa" in disguise,' said Mel. 'And, the answers she has given made us realise that as a mother tree, she cares deeply for you all and would look after your safety.'

'There was one more thing,' said Mikal. 'She forgot to wipe off her trunk-coloured lipstick - that was definitely a noticeable clue.'

The honorary tree smiled at them and then suddenly, a number of trees from the orchard that were clapping and smiling surrounded the boys.

The boys realised then that the orchard grounds was not an orchard at all, it was an ancient conference site. An ancient, power of nature embedded in their roots, gave them the ability to uproot themselves and travel invisibly to the conference site.

'Well done you've solved the puzzle! Guess you will want to be leaving now and you have my permission. By the way, my name is Baye. I am known as Reye Baye, (meaning "Big Father"), because of my size. 'Being the second eldest and tallest, here, I'm really surprised that I wasn't called up for questioning like the others,' he joked. 'Anyway, it's time for you to go. Just don't go dropping into my branches anytime soon,' he added and shook their hands.

As they shook hands, Mel realised they were on the same grounds as they were before. He was about to mention it, when a "whooshing" sound; brought them back to swinging on the protruding branches of the Mango Papaya tree,

'We're back in 1962,' they said and immediately winced from the sting of the scratches on their backs as Elmstead and Birchard came to their rescue.

Birchard mixed green sap with crushed herbs and applied this to their bruises; stating that there are plants and herbs for every ailment. Later with their bruises miraculously healed, the boys explained all to their magic trees, who swore blind they had nothing to do with their disappearance. In fact they hadn't even realised they were missing. They were gone for a few seconds in 1962, but for several hours in an alternate reality.

Just before take-off, the boys spotted a familiar tree they

had not seen in that spot on the ground before. 'It's the Kilifa,' they whispered and ran to embrace her.

'I am still here a century later my clever little English Wackies, even though to you it took only a few seconds. Another hundred years and my time will probably end.'

'We're really glad to see you once again. We didn't get to say goodbye before been "swished" back here to 1962.'

On the other side of the field, sure enough there was Baye, the giant tree. He had stayed on the grounds to protect the Kilifa, and bear fruits like the mango papaya tree they had fallen off before. As he had guessed, they were related after all! Baye saluted them and the boys did the same and hugged him.

Then they saw Kenja. Why hadn't they noticed before, Kenja had saved them from falling!

Kenja smiled and said, 'I'm the Ranking Mango Kent Prince of this field. I didn't reveal my identity as your quiz assistant, but I knew you clever guys would figure it out.'

The boys hugged Kenja and introduced them all to the magic trees, who felt honoured to meet these Ancients. Some day they hope to evolve just like them.

৯Chapter 16: The Manuscript৶

The vortex miraculously appeared and minutes later they were safely transported back to their Grandparents' garden. Mel glanced at his watch; it was precisely 12 noon.

'Woooow ...unbelievable!' was all he could say.

'You two look a right mess...have you been rummaging around a building site?' said Grandma Cee

'Building site?' the boys replied grinning from ear to ear. 'Oh no Grandma, we've been on a magnificent adventure, you just wouldn't believe it.'

Grandma Cee rolled her eyes and sighed. 'Oh lord help us!' she said. 'My grandsons are delusional.'

The boys could hardly sleep that night from excitement. They were lying in bed thinking about Gambia and their next adventure in Jamaica, and decided to get a drink from the kitchen. A light was on in the study near the stairs and the boys noticed a manuscript on the table.

Mel recalled hearing their Grandpa saying Grandma Cee was writing a book. 'Mary, one of her workmates, gave her a note pad and pen to start writing,' he had said. 'Come to think of it, I gave her a note pad too. She said the pen writes like magic, but she has been writing the book for over two years now and it's still not finished.'

'Let's have a look,' said Mikal.

Flicking through, they were surprised to find that it was a children's book, and there was something familiar about the chapter titles.

'I didn't know Grandma was into writing fiction. Who would have thought that! I don't think she would like anyone sneaking a peek through it though.'

'We had better keep it a secret then Mikal, but I can't wait to tell our friends about our magic trees. Do you think Jamaica is the same as Africa?'

'I don't know, some Jamaicans had ancestors from Africa, so maybe they are not that different.'

'Cool, perhaps the mangoes are the same too!' said Mel, as he yawned, snuggled up under the covers and drifted off to sleep.

Breakfast is served

They awoke to the lovely smell of breakfast -fish fingers, omelette and beans. 'I was just thinking Grandma, what did you have for breakfast in Jamaica?' said Mel.

'Hmmm ... I had either cornmeal porridge, plantain with fried dumplings and eggs, or roast breadfruit with calaloo or with ackee and saltfish.'

'Breadfruit is a type of bread that tastes like fruit; isn't it?'

Grandma Cee laughed, 'No Mel it's a green vegetable; round like a ball and grows on trees.'

'What about breakfast in the Gambia Grandpa?'

'I ate Ruy; a type of porridge and French bread with eggs and ham, which you're Grandma won't let me eat now. You'd need to go to Gambia to taste these delicious dishes.'

'Maybe we've already been - in our dreams!' said Mel.

Grandpa Dee shook his head. 'Oh really, you boys certainly know how to let your imagination run wild, don't you!'

Chapter 18: The Jamaican Beach Hotel

Birchard and Elmstead arrived in the garden in a gust of wind looking quite cheerful, and found Mel and Mikal waiting; raring to go on their next adventure.

Before lift-off, they had to agree not to wander off without permission. When they were all set, the magic trees ascended, and did their spinning ritual like before to enter the dazzling vortex.

In a matter of minutes, they landed near a grand looking hotel, on a white sandy beach that seemed to stretch from one end of the coast to the other. It had an amazing view of the clear blue sea, which the boys had never seen before.

Tourists from all walks of life were soaking up the sun in an attempt to get a tan. Speedboats with streaming waves filled the sea, whilst security guards - the only ones fully dressed- patrolled the beachfront looking for intruders.

'This is Negril Beach in Jamaica,' said Elmstead, 'The third largest island in the Caribbean and probably the most beautiful. We'll take a trip to the family village later, but for now, enjoy yourselves ...have some fun ... go for a swim; or do cartwheels on the beach, but just steer clear of the security guards - you got that!'

Mel and Mikal did all the fun things that Birchard encouraged them to do, except the swimming - they would have to ditch their capes for that! However, it wasn't long before their curiosity reared its head and they sneaked off to explore the hotel's grand interior.

Once inside this impressive building, boasting a plush reception area with marbled floors, they mischievously went up and down the huge silver lifts, positioned on either side of an exquisitely, carved staircase, leading to all floors.

They played with the lift buttons, alarming the guests and followed some into their luxurious rooms. To them, it was hilarious when guests were startled seeing their TVs being switched on and off, paintings hanging on delicately painted pink walls swinging from side to side and cupboard doors mysteriously opening and shutting.

One of the guests - a Spanish woman who spoke very fast - was not the type to succumb to fright because of a few eerie happenings. She dialled the receptionist, who promised to send someone to investigate. Then she locked the door, put on a summer dress in a colour to match her fiery temper and waited for the investigator to arrive.

'Uh oh! I think we have gone too far Mel. We can't walk through those locked doors.'

Before long, there was a knock on the door and the woman opened it, with a look of determination on her face that said, *Yes, I am going to get this problem sorted!* A skinny man wearing the hotel's uniform walked in. He was fairly, short with a friendly face, and deeply tanned. Behind him stood another entity that was totally the opposite, tall, stocky and angry looking.

Dressed in a red shirt, black trousers and red scarf around his waist, he stared at the boys, like a bull about to charge. Then he headed straight to where they were, with his black fringe bouncing off his forehead, whilst the other man addressed the Spanish woman in a polite, business-like Jamaican accent.

'I am Alfred, the Duty Manager. You called about some disturbance, what is the problem madam?'

'Yes, come in Alfred,' she replied proudly, swishing the hem of her summer dress as she walked away from the door. 'I'm Catalina Torres. Have I been allocated a haunted room, or, is there some sort of a prank going on here?'

'Certainly not Madam, what do you ask that?'

'Things are moving about; my bed sheets are flying up and down in the air - what is this?'

'I don't know Madam. We have never had this problem before in any of the hotel rooms. Perhaps it's a bit of wind blowing through the window.'

'Are you blind ... can't you see that the windows are closed. The air conditioning is actually on.'

'Sorry Madam, let me put my glasses on and have a look. Maybe something else could be creating the problem.'

The tall angry man by now was standing in front of Mel and Mikal. Looking down on them, he shouted in the same accent as the Spanish woman, 'You are the problem!' 'What are you doing here? Get out!'

'He can see us,' said Mel.

'But we've got our capes on,' replied Mikal, 'and, he's not a dog, monkey or hyena.'

The man flew into a rage. 'What did you say? Are you calling me a dog or monkey? Do I look like them to you?' He grabbed them by their T-shirts and lifted them up in the air. No ... no ... wait,' said Mikal. 'We are invisible - we have invisible capes ... we meant that you should not be able to see us like dogs and ...'

'Shut up you winging sprite!' He roared.

Mikal realised then that the other people in the room couldn't hear him - they were continuing their conversation and investigation as normal. 'Who are you?' Mikal asked.

'Why don't you put us down and tell us who you are?' said Mel in support of his cousin.

'Why do you wanna know eh? I'm Carlos and she,' he pointed to Catalina, 'is my wife!' He let go of their T-shirts and watched them tumble to the floor.

'But it doesn't look like she can see you,' said Mel.

'Of course not ... I'm dead!'

'Dead ... you're ... you're dead ... oh boy!' Mikal tried to think of what else to say whilst Mel hid behind him. They had never seen a ghost before and both felt like pinching themselves.

'So ... so ... why ... why are you here? Where's your grave yard?' he asked, less boldly than he would normally.

'Why am I here? You dare to ask,' he roared again. 'Can't you see that I'm her security guard? I protect her from scoundrels like you. You must be trying to find her priceless gold, buried over a hundred years ago in a Spaniard Jar. Only I know of its whereabouts,' he sneered.

Mikal got really, upset. 'Scoundrel ... that's the same as a "villain" isn't it? We aren't scoundrels or villains,' he said angrily. 'We're decent young people, just having a bit of harmless fun - our magic trees told us to have fun.'

'Trees ... what trees?' said Carlos. 'It's one thing talking to a ghost, but quite another thing if you're talking to trees that can't see or hear you.'

'Well our magic trees can,' said Mikal.

'That's it,' Carlos said angrily. 'I'm throwing you crazy sprites out of here right now!'

He grabbed them by their T-shirts and marched them towards the door, yelling for him to let them go. The door opened with unseen hands to the Duty Manager's amazement, and somehow the boys managed to wriggle free when he passed through the door.

They escaped along the corridor and ran towards the lift. 'Come on, come on!' Mikal said to the lift that seemed to be in no hurry to get to the seventh floor. Entering the lift, Mikal pushed the button for the ground floor. They both watched the door closed and then slid to the floor in relief.

The indicator showed 7th, 6th and 5th floor, then suddenly, there was a loud "clank" and the lights flickered on and off eerily.

'What's happening? It's stopped moving!' said Mel.

Mikal pushed the lift buttons several times. Nothing happened. He tried using both hands to pull open the lift doors, but that didn't work either - it was stuck! He pushed the button to set off the alarm and it rang piercingly.

As they stared at the door waiting to be rescued, the middle started to protrude slowly into a point. Their eyes focused on the protruding point, growing bigger and bigger, making both edges of the lift door, fold back on itself.

A head with thick black hair, proceeded to push through and to their horror, they recognised the face. Carlos had found them! His head pushed right through the fabric of the door and he stared at them with a wide grin. The boys shuffled to the back of the lift to give him room.

'There is nowhere to hide buddies. I can squeeze through any surface in seconds, because as a matter of fact, I am just gas. Hahaha! Let me assist you,' he said above the sound of the alarm. His long detached finger glided through the lift, pushed the alarm button and then vanished.

The lift began to move with his head still poking through the door. The indicator said 6th then 7th floor. It was going back to where they had started.

They were getting ready to rush through the lift door at the sound of the "ping" but Carlos beat them to it. He lifted them up by the collar. 'You scum how you dare wander around my hotel scaring my wife.'

Mikal's face was flushed with anger. 'We're not scum, scoundrel or villains,' he said staring into Carlos' face. He lifted his foot and aimed a bit lower than Carlos' groin. His foot went right through Carlos' body, but somehow Carlos still felt the pain.

'Ouch, you thug!' Carlos yelled.

Mikal aimed his foot and repeated the attack. 'I'm not a "thug" either. My name is Mikal,' he pointed to Mel, 'and this is my cousin Mel.'

Carlos flew into another rage and held Mikal up in the air. 'I am going to personally, throw you off these premises and ...' he stopped in mid flow when he felt a tap on his shoulder.

A voice from behind that was much deeper than his own said, 'Going somewhere bullfighter?' Carlos turned around to face Birchard and Elmstead peering down at him with folded arms. Being much taller, they were literally bending over him; it was a good thing the hotel had high ceilings.

From the look on Carlos' face, it was clear that he was quite taken back by what he thought were two unfamiliar apparitions. 'Who are you and, what are you doing in my hotel?' he asked with a feeble tone of authority.

'I think your haunting days are over - don't you!' said Elmstead. 'Now ... let us assist you with your load. You see, you're holding our two friends, and just so you know, we are their security guards.'

'That's right! We protect them from scoundrels or should we say "villains" like you,' said Birchard. 'So go on ... go and wave your red scarf at other bulls. These are pretty, harmless - they do not want your wife's gold -they have never even seen or heard of a Spaniard Jar.'

The magic trees drew their leafy faces with puckered brows to Carlos' face and looked him straight in the eye. At that point, the boys felt a cold breeze moving swiftly through the corridor.

They found themselves falling to the ground and when they looked up, Carlos had disappeared, leaving only his red scarf on the spot where he had stood.

Meanwhile, the Duty Manager was still trying to get Catalina to accept his explanation of the problem, when they felt the cold breeze.

'Ah, told you it was the wind Madam! You are on the top floor. It comes straight along the corridor and under the door. Whoosh!' he gestured with his arms.

He left Catalina pondering on this, and on the way passed the lift, picked up the red scarf. 'Crazy woman;' he muttered. 'Dat was a waste a time. Mi know sey dere was no duppee inna de room.'

'Well I guess Carlos was right about one thing,' said Birchard. 'He is a real ghost, or should we say, "just gas" Hahaha!'

$\mathcal{M}$el and Mikal were in the air again lapping up the cool sea breeze that took their breath away, as it seem to playfully brush against their faces.

Below, big fancy houses and small rundown shacks, dangling washing from clotheslines, dotted the scenery. There were many shops and street traders, and some travellers with baskets carefully balanced on their heads, rushed to the safety of the grass verge as cars sped by.

They flew above a winding road to get to their Great, Great, Great Grandparents land in the village of Rock Spring. Interestingly, a crooked coconut tree, littered with coconuts beneath it, marked the entrance and Mel instantly imagined giant hands bending it into its crooked shape. *Ouch!*

No one was at home in the cottage that was badly in need of a coat of paint, so Mikal decided to narrate

Grandma Cee's tales of the village that she was familiar with as a child.

'There was no street lights in those days, but the villagers never got lost travelling in the dark, or felt scared of the night sounds. Some nights Grandma huddled on the veranda with her cousins, listening to her Great Grandparents strange night tales.

There was one about a horse with fiery eyes and a rolling calf that chased people with bells jingling around its neck.'

'A rolling calf ... what's that?'

'Don't know Mel, it is probably the ghost of a baby cow. But, after the night tales, they were all too afraid to get water from the tank to wash before going to bed.'

'Gosh, I would be scared too,' said Mel, 'But Grandma said not to be scared of the dark. It's difficult to see, but things are exactly the same as when the lights are on.'

'That's true,' said Elmstead, 'us trees sway with the wind under the moonlight until dawn; watching rodents and insects crawling around and listening to strange sounds, but we're never scared.'

'Oh hush Elmstead. I hear you shaking in your roots sometimes when you think I'm not listening.'

'No I don't Birchard!'

'Oh yes you do.'

'Ok guys that's enough! You're making us feel scared now.'

'Come on Mel ...thought you said you were brave,' said Elmstead. 'Those folk tales aren't true ... if the trees here could talk, they would confirm this.'

'Your Grandma was right,' said Birchard. 'You should never be scared of the dark, because too much light can be blinding and you would definitely have to get some specs. Hahaha!'

*Q*fter the story telling, Mikal sat under the crooked coconut tree, visualising how the family land might have looked in the past.

The scorching sun shone high in the sky and a fascinating haze began to form in the distance. It was slowly spreading towards him and Mikal couldn't keep his eyes off it. He was mesmerised and the soaring temperature made him feel like steam was pouring out of his pores.

Soon he felt soothed by a gentle sea breeze; heard waves splashing against rocks and even felt sand between his toes. He looked away from the hazy scene and to his amazement; he was on a deserted beach.

He gasped as a large, strange stone object, presumably guarding the beach, stared back at him, with features resembling the Star Wars character, Jabba the Hut. Looking around Mikal frantically questioned how he had arrived there and then something odd caught his eye.

Hiding behind a rock, he watched as a strange group of scantily dressed, dark skinned people with straight black hair, dragged a small boat with queer looking sails onto the beach. More followed from the boats behind, hauling their few belongings.

He heard footsteps crunching in the sand, someone approaching from behind. Before he could turn around, someone grabbed him roughly by the shoulders and tried to pull him to his feet.

The person shouted something to the others in a strange language, probably alerting them to the intruder in their midst. Mikal struggled to free himself from his strong grip, but could not summon up the energy to do so. He moved in slow motion; his feet felt like lead and when he opened his mouth to scream nothing came out.

He tried to say, 'Leave me alone,' but the words were stuck in his throat. He struggled to push the person away with arms that felt so heavy he could hardly lift them.

'Help ... help me!' He finally managed to squeak.

Then he heard someone calling his name. 'Mikal ... wake up, it's alright now ... wake up!'

Mikal jumped up startled to see Mel standing over him. 'What! What's happening ...where am I?' he asked.

'Right here with the rest of us,' replied Mel

'I must have been dreaming,' said Mikal.

I've heard that before, thought Mel. 'Dreaming about what?'

'Strange people on a beach, one of them tried to capture me and then I heard someone calling.'

'That was me. You'd fallen asleep under the tree. You must have been dreaming about those sunbathers at Negril Beach.'

'No Mel, these people were different ...' Mikal paused, hoping that Mel would grasp what he was saying, but his blank expression confirmed that he didn't. 'Oh never mind, maybe it was just a silly dream.'

'Mikal you look dazed, are you ok,' said Elmstead.

'Yes, I'm fine. It's probably the heat. Think I'd better get up before I doze off again.'

'That's a good idea. We certainly didn't fly you all the way here to sleep,' replied Elmstead.

When Mikal recovered from his dream, both he and Mel had questions like, 'Who were the first inhabitants of Jamaica, was it Africans?'

'No, it was the Tainos or Arawaks as they are often called,' replied Elmstead. 'They came from Guyana in South America and settled here 2,500 years before Christopher Columbus came in 1494.'

'Really! Did they look like Africans?'

'No, they looked more like dark skinned Indians. '

Mikal went strangely quiet when he heard this. *It can't be,* he thought. *It was just a stupid dream!*

'Are you alright Mikal?' Elmstead asked again.

'Yeah, I am fine - just feeling a bit hot.'

'So how did Africans get here?' Mel continued.

'They were brought here from Africa. Some of their descendants still live here in Maroon Town; and people from India and China have settled here too.

'Maroon Town -I am going to go there one day,' said Mikal. 'And if it exist, I will find that deserted beach,' he quietly muttered.

'Jamaica looks like a great place Elmstead, what else can you tell us about it?' asked Mel.

'Have you heard of the Blue Mountains, towering above the island at 7402 feet high? The finest coffee beans in the world are grown there.'

'7402 feet high! I'd love to climb to the top and view the whole country with my binoculars.'

'Sounds like you're itching for more adventure Mel and the Blue Mountains of Jamaica, might just be the place to do that. Anyway, I forgot to mention that terrible earthquake that destroyed Port Royal in 1692. You know Birchard; flicking through my history bank, I still imagine that I can hear those people crying out for help.'

'Ok, enough of that Elmstead. Let's move on to a happier note like reggae music that was originated here.' Birchard made a silly attempt to dance with his stiff knees as he sung, 'Lively up yourself and don't be no drag, lively up yourself …. Bet you feel like dancing now Mel!'

'Yeah, but I will do it later. Grandpa said that there is a time and place for everything.'

'Excuse me!' said Birchard, feeling like he had suddenly shrunk to three feet tall. 'I think I'll leave Elmstead to continue.'

Some yards away from the cottage, they found trees with plantains and breadfruits.

Mel wasn't sure about eating breadfruits, but he thought they would score a great goal, and attempted to prove this by kicking one into an area that resembled a bushy goal post.

Further on, the boys found mangoes with funny names like Graham, Julie and Bombay.

'Try them!' They are really delicious, and some of your Grandma's favourite mangoes,' said Elmstead.

'Listen guys, what do you think about time travelling? '

'Time travel - in a time machine - do you have one?'

'Well, something like that!'

If you wish, we could take you back to the time when your ancestors existed here.'

'Sounds awesome!' said Mel.

ᗰel and Mikal agreed to explore the area and not wander off too far. Strolling passed a field with rows of cane, the boys tried to imagine how they convert them into sugar, when Jamaica was the world's biggest sugar producer.

They also went passed a mound of bauxite rocks that are transformed into to aluminium to make things like pots, tins and aeroplane parts. Interestingly, the colour of the rocks was similar to the dusty, Gambian roads.

'Let's just keep away from those rocks Mikal; I don't want any red colouring on my trainers this time.'

They were watching birds flying in and out of trees and shrubs, when they heard an unidentified sound and went to investigate. Flying around an exotic looking flower, were two beautiful tiny birds, with wings flapping so fast, they were hardly visible.

The boys moved nearer to get a closer look and to their surprise one of them hovered over their out-stretched

palms as if it was expecting to be fed.

It was really a remarkable sight and being so near, the boys could truly admire its unique form. 'I wonder what type of bird this is,' Mel whispered, so as not to scare it.

'Maybe it's the national bird, Grandma said something about it,' Mikal whispered back. 'It's making a strange humming sound with its wings.'

'Hmmm, a bird that hums, a "humming bird" that sounds so cool!' said Mel.

'I like its beautiful streaming tail, green feathers and red beak I'm gonna call it a Red-beaked Streamer Tail bird.'

'I'm sticking with "Humming Bird" it sounds better. I can't wait to tell Grandma Cee all about it.'

'Uh oh! You'd get us into serious trouble Mel.'

They followed the enchanting humming birds, flitting from flower to flower until they were out of sight and soon a swishing sound filled the air. As they got nearer, they could see that the sound was coming from a winding stream that seemed to stretch forever.

Shrubs and small trees decorated its banks and a few people went by with baskets on their heads, unaware of the invisible intruders about to investigate their local stream.

'Let's paddle .through and see where .it flows. 'I don't think we should Mikal. The trees told us not to wander off too far and I can't swim.'

'Oh come on you don't have to swim - just paddle.'

Mel eventually gave in, and they hid their trainers and capes under a shrub before entering the stream.

In the stream, tiny odd-looking crabs with shells fused onto their backs crawled on the rocks, cleansed by the stream's constant flow. They almost looked like they were marching. *Solider Crabs*, Mel thought.

The soothing surge of warm water massaging their feet distracted them from the fact that the stream was getting deeper the further they went.

Mel tried to catch a colourful fish, but its scaly body slipped easily through his hands. He reached for a crab with a shell on its back and it nipped his fingers. Struggling to shake it off, he lost his footing and fell.

He realised then that what had started out as a stream had now turned into a river. It was now much wider than its starting point, and pulling him swiftly towards its deep end.

'Mikal, help ... help,' he shouted above the rushing sound of the river. Mikal was paddling further out when he heard Mel's shout for help, and turned around just in time to see his head going under the water.

Mel rose again gasping for air but could not stay afloat. The more he panicked, the harder he found it to raise above the water rapidly submerging him; until eventually he passed out and floated along with the swift current.

'Mel, Mel ... hold on, I am coming, where are you?'

Unlike Mel, he was a good swimmer, having won several medals at school. He swam to where he last saw him and frantically dived in and out of the water, calling his name repeatedly, but there was no response.

The thought of something happening to Mel and

possibly not returning home filled him with dread. Mikal shouted for help, but it was a waste of time; no one heard, even though he was now visible.

A piece of cloth on the riverbank caught his attention, and he swam quickly to the spot, fearing the worst. His heart skipped a beat when he saw Mel slumped on the ground. He turned him over to check his breathing and jumped back in dismay, as at first he didn't appear to be. Instead, he looked lifeless and pale - he needed help!

He remembered seeing a paramedic on TV resuscitating someone and thought he would try it. He had to do something to save him!

He blew into Mel's mouth and pressed his chest with his palms several times. Eventually Mel stirred and coughed a little, but his eyes remained closed and he drifted back to how he was before, looking like he was hardly breathing.

Mikal tried again until he was almost out of breath. Mel stirred, then coughed and water dribbled from his mouth. Mikal turned him on his side as more spewed out, but Mel still looked poorly and he wasn't sure what else to do, or how to get him back to where they had left the magic trees

'Someone help me please. Jesus, Jehovah, Allah, The

Most High whatever you're called, save him please,' he cried out. Mikal was about to give up when he heard rustling in the surrounding shrubs; someone or something was approaching. He crouched low and anxiously waited to see who, or what would emerge from the bushes.

Suddenly a large wild goat with the longest horns he had ever seen, rushed out of the bushes at great speed, followed closely by another. Mikal was quite taken aback; he had seen pictures of goats before but never any like these.

They ran around the edge of the stream, heading towards him. At first, he thought they were going to attack him like the dogs and Hyenas, especially as he was now visible, but he soon realised that they were running from something.

The goats ran within a few yards from where he knelt over Mel; then suddenly changed direction when they spotted him. Seconds later, he heard what he thought the goats might have been running from.

The sound of the approaching stranger or thing felt so near Mikal could hardly breathe from the anxiety, and at that point, he wished he had their invisible capes. A hush came over the riverbed; all the peculiar noises ceased and even the stream for once was still.

He closed his eyes; feeling too scared to look at what might next materialise out of the shrubs; and hoped that whatever it was, would run off like the goats. Then he jumped and stifled a scream, as large hands brushed against his shoulders.

'Mikal are you all right? What on earth has happened here?' Hearing Elmstead's voice and seeing them both, was such a relief, he fell to his knees and clasped his hands as if in prayer.

'Thank goodness! I am so glad to see you, he said franticly. I thought it was a ... thought it was a ...'

'Oh never mind all that,' said Birchard. 'What has happened to Mel?'

Mikal frantically tried to explain. 'He fell into the stream; it pulled him away... he's not breathing. I tried to make him breathe, but couldn't ... help him please,' he pleaded.'

Both trees rushed to Mel's side, and Birchard who had knowledge of First Aid attended to him. He was breathing shallow but steadily. Mikal had done a better job than he had thought.

Birchard blew a pure source of oxygen into his lungs and Mel stirred and coughed several times before his lungs were working fully to improve his breathing.

'Mel, you're alive!' Mikal cried out. 'I'm so sorry, you disappeared under the water, and then I found you on the riverbank. I blew into your lungs ... and ... and...' Mikal got so emotional that he started to sob again.

'Don't worry everything will be all right,' said Elmstead. 'Things could have been a lot worse. Luckily, we heard your cry for help on the ridge of the winds. Come on, let's collect your things and get Mel to a sunnier spot.'

With Mel tucked up in Birchard's branches. They flew back to the family grounds and placed him on a bed of leaves in the sun.

As the sun blazed above their heads, they sipped coconut juice from a fresh coconut, to quench their thirst, whilst waiting for Mel's clothes to dry out.

'Love you cuz,' Mel said feebly in between sips. 'But next time I won't follow you to places we shouldn't go.'

He smiled faintly when Mikal said, 'That's alright Mel, next time I won't ask if you're not brave enough to follow.'

$\mathcal{M}$el and Mikal paced up and down anxiously, waiting for Birchard and Elmstead's decision. After the "rule breaking" incident at the stream, the trees almost cancelled their time travel plans. Finally, they decided the boys had learnt their lesson and it would go ahead as planned.

It was important for the boys to close their eyes and focus on the year 1962, but this was difficult. Things were popping in an out of their minds, and being curious, they couldn't help peeking at the magic trees opening up a concealed flap in their trunks.

Rotating within their trunks was a blue disc surrounded by triangles with illuminated edges that did not seem to be directly connected to the centre and it bleeped like a submarine sonar signal.

'What's that?' Mel whispered to Mikal.

'It's a Time Travel Compass,' said Elmstead, who could

hear even their slightest whisper.

'That's awesome, can I try it.'

'Not on your life,' said Elmstead.

He clicked the compass switch and all around them, things slowly started to swirl. Before they knew what was happening, they were transported fifty years in the past. Just on time for their Great, Great, Great Grandparents, Mathias and Vashti's wedding anniversary.

The scenery was astonishingly different. Quite clearly, they were standing in the same place, but it was as if a completely new world had opened up. Everything looked fresh and vibrant. The place was alive! The land looked rich and fertile. The grass was greener; flowerbeds glistened with colours and the hedge looked as if Edward Scissorhands had paid it a visit.

Surprisingly the crooked coconut tree was straight, and as for the mango trees, their branches were laden with fruits, begging to be plucked. Old-school music blared out from a radio in the cottage that now looked as pretty as a picture with its fresh coat of yellow paint.

Young Grandma Cee wore a frilly, blue dress and her plaits with hair clips at the end, swung from side to side. She skipped happily with her cousins; Juanita, Pauline and Mansie, who were always up for a laugh, and his brother Barry who could wiggled his ears like Dr Spock. As they watched, the boys found it hard to believe that she was once so jolly and carefree.

Looking around, Mel took an interest in the beautiful national flower - The Lignum Vitae - and the national tree called The Blue Mahoe, growing near the cottage.

'So, Jamaica has a national flower, tree and bird, are there any more "national" things?' he asked

'You can add three more; the national flag, the national anthem and the delicious national dish -Ackee and Saltfish,' said Elmstead.

'Hmmm ... that's a lot of nationals, but I think I want to have a taste of that national dish.'

In the outdoor kitchen their Great Ancestor Mathias; an excellent chef who loved to peacefully smoke his pipe, and Great Ancestor Vashti who lived to be a hundred years old, tended the Dutch pots simmering on coal stoves, and the lovely aroma lured the boys to the entrance.

As they stood there, Great Ancestor Vashti stared blankly in their direction, as if sensing a presence. Mikal couldn't help noticing that with her dark complexion and headscarf, she looked very similar to the picture of Grandpa Dee's mum.

When the feast was prepared, all the family members, including Mel and Mikal's great, great, great, aunt and uncles, sat down to dine around the table laid out in the yard, and the boys couldn't resist nibbling some of the delicious food.

Quite unexpectedly, Mel's cape got caught on the edge of the table. It fell from his shoulders, leaving him completely visible in an era that he didn't belong with a mouthful of rice and peas. Their Great, Great Grandma Ella; dressed like a very attractive, wealthy woman, with dark brown complexion, leapt from her seat.

'Huh! Who are you?' she said. 'I don't recognise you. Where yuh spring from and why yuh eating our food?'

The whole family turned their attention to Mel and at that moment he didn't know whether to run or come clean.

'I'm ... I'm ... very sorry -I didn't mean to alarm you.' He paused briefly and then boldly said, 'Well, I suppose I will have to explain this the hard way. My name is Mel. You might not believe me, but I'm your relative from the future.'

'Fram de future? What yuh mean?' said Great, Great, Great Grandma Vashti, in a Jamaican dialect. She had completely missed the point about him being a relative.

At this point, Mikal threw off his cape and she couldn't believe her eyes. Pushing her headscarf forward on her forehead she said, 'Now dere's two of dem! What is dis?'

'What's your name?' her daughter - Great, Great, Grandma Ella, asked.

'Mikal cleared the lump in his throat. 'My name is Mikal. We're so sorry; we didn't mean to scare you.'

'Yuh didn't mean to scare us! A suppose yuh going to tell me de same nonsense about de future,' she responded.

'I'm sorry to say this, but it's true. We're from England, in the year 2012.'

'What! Boy ... yuh tink we stupid?' said her brother, their Great, Great, Great, Uncle Victor. He was a skilled electrician, who judging by the way he was dressed, seemed quite well off. 'Where's yuh mother?' he said, mopping his brow with a handkerchief. 'She live round ere?'

'No, she's not here ... I left her in England in 2012.'

His brother, their Great, Great, Great Uncle Sonny joined in. Mikal guessed he was a farmer, from his wellington boots and the cutlass near his chair. 'Boy stap yuh stupidness,' he said. 'Dis is 1962, so how could you two leave yuh mother in 2012 or come fram dere; das a long way hafe -I'll be dead by then,' he joked.

The children including young Grandma Cee started giggling. 'Dem must be crazy,' they whispered.

Grandma Cee's mum, their Great Grandma Millicent decided to speak up. 'Maybe dem telling de truth; sometimes strange tings appen you nuh. Wi don't always hander stand all de tings dat goes on in dis world.'

'Don't talk foolishness,' said her sister, Great, Great Aunt Blanche; a dark skinned woman, quite strong in character and very striking in her looks. 'What strange tings yuh talking habout. De only ting I notice, is dat dem talk with an English accent. And, come to tink of it, yes, dem look a bit like de family - isn't it Mama?'

'A suppose suh,' Great, Great Grandma Ella replied.

'I tink suh too,' said Ella's younger sister, Rubena. Ella's other daughter, their Great Grandma Millicent, who was also a strong, silent character, was quietly observing them from where she sat. They knew her quite well in their own time.

'Where yuh sey your mother is?' she asked.

'She's at home in England,' Mikal replied, lowering his eyes she noted her beauty. Then he let it slip. 'But our Grandma is here.' Elmstead and Birchard cringed when they heard this.

'Yuh Grandma is ere,' she replied, 'Where ... where is she? Mi can't see her.' Mel had no choice but to point his finger directly at young Grandma Cee.

'That's her there!' Grandma Cee froze, and the other children stared at her with gaping mouths.

'Me!' she replied when she had composed herself. 'I don't know yuh, I'm only seven, suh ow can I be yuh Grandma - boy yuh crazy?'

Mel smiled as he said, 'You don't know us now, but you will in the future. In fact, we really love your delicious, carrot cakes and fish pies.'

'Fish pie, what fish pie...' me can't even cook!' She

looked at her Great Aunt Rubena, 'Please talk to dis boy aunty I tink he's mad.'

Great, Great, Great, Ancestor Mathias who had remained quiet up until then, interrupted. 'Dis is certainly a strange day. Dere is four generations ere, possible five if we count dese two, and I ave a strange feeling habout all dis. So, let's jus welcome dem and henjoy de feast. Come on ... give dem some of de national dish, wid roast breadfruit. If they're one of us, dey will love it!'

Mel and Mikal joined in the feast and chatted with everyone around the table, who explained the family connections, even though they still doubted their story about being from the future. Before leaving, all the family members hugged and kissed them.

When it was Grandma Cee's turn, she hesitated, then smiled and hugged them both before she quietly asked, 'Tell mi someting, carrot cake ... does it tase de same as rum cake?'

As Mel and Mikal said their goodbyes and left their family, they noticed grey clouds appearing in the distance and within minutes, it began to rain. Lightning flashed and on the third flash, an image suddenly appeared between the trees. They saw people seated in rows of chairs in front of a mixed raced man with a moustache. His neatly trimmed hair parted to the side, framed his handsome face and he was immaculately dressed in a navy blue suit and tie. *Isn't he hot?* Mel and Mikal thought.

The congregation listened as he preached, clapping and nodding to every word, but something was strange about the scene - they weren't getting wet! Unbelievably, the rain was falling everywhere, except where they sat. Mel and Mikal couldn't figure out how this sort of thing could happen, but when Birchard strolled off with a mischievous glint in his eyes, they suddenly remembered.

'Huh! It's the miracle man,' they yelled. 'Our Great, Granddad Harold, at his Miracle Sermon that Grandma Cee told us about. How did the trees know about this?'

'Like they always do Mel - they access it through our thoughts!'

In the excitement, they smacked their palms together for a high five and yelled, 'Great, Granddad Harold; was simply amazing!'

'Legendary!' said Mikal.

❧Chapter 24: The Outhouse❧

$\mathcal{T}$he water drain stretched from the roof to a barrel, conveniently positioned at the side of the house.

'Check this out!' said Birchard. 'I think this is where the children washed their feet after the night tales and that outhouse at the far end, must be a loo.

'A loo, don't they have this indoors?' Mel asked.

'They are built separately in these days, like the kitchen.'

'Can I use it? I really want to pee.'

'Go ahead Mikal, but be quick, we have to leave soon.'

Mikal walked towards the loo with some uneasiness. He tugged on the door and it opened with a prolonged, eerie, squeak. Inside the small, squared room, an unlit lamp hung on the door and a raised, mahogany seating area, smelling strongly of wood polish, stretched along the length of the wall. There was no sign of a flushing handle like modern loos, so Mikal figured there must be a camouflaged lid or opening somewhere. He searched for this in the dimness; and peered inside, and to his surprise the loo, was a deep hole in the ground - a mere pit! The smell rose to his nostrils, but as he desperately wanted to pee, he ignored the urge to slam the lid shut.

Pulling down his pants, he aimed for the centre, but soon realised the noise of his pee, had alerted something near the window. He almost ran out with his pants down, but instead peered through the dimness to see what it was.

Whatever it was jumped from the window onto the dimly lit, mahogany seated area in one swoop; landing with a slight thud. Mikal zipped up his pants to rush out then stopped, as he felt something was watching him. A bit of sunlight shone through the window near the ceiling onto a creepy looking green lizard, extending and withdrawing a flap of skin near his throat.

Mikal stared briefly into its eyes and for some reason, imagined it stretching to the height of the ceiling, with the flap expanding like a huge balloon, before it spoke in patois. *'Wha yuh doing ere, dis is my spot buddy... get hout!'*

Mikal's shriek alerted another lizard, perched above the door, and one above the window. They were all looking curiously at him, with their tiny peculiar heads leaning to one side. He grabbed the doorknob to run out and at the same time, the lizard above the door jumped off.

His cold green tail brushed against Mikal's forehead as it scurried down his back. Mikal panicked and ran out yelling, 'Get it off! I hate lizards. Get that ugly thing off my back!'

Birchard flicked off the small green lizard scurrying down the back of Mikal's T-shirt and said, 'What's the problem? It's just a lizard; probably more frightened of you than you were of it.'

'But it was dim and smelly and there was a huge ...'

'Oh come on Mikal. It's just an outdoor loo… not a luxury, indoor toilet. If you were living here in these times without either one, you would have to relieve yourself in the bushes,' Birchard said amusingly.

'What … no way!' In an instant, Mikal actually pictured himself doing so with his bare bottom and other parts, left to the mercy of stinging nettles and all sorts of prickly bushes. The look on Mikal's face said it all.

'Come on,' said Birchard. 'Go and wash your hands and let's leave, before your imagination gets out of hand.'

*H*aving had the chance to see some of their ancestors the boys accepted the offer of another trip into the past before heading home.

Once again they were watching the time travel compass being activated and did not focus on the era. At first, everything seemed normal apart from the bleeping compass; then things changed and time fascinatingly accelerated all around them.

Night and day passed in seconds; speeding up the hours, days, months and years. Clouds quickly drifted in and drifted out. Seeds grew rapidly into trees and plants, and flowers sprouted, bloomed and then disappeared from view.

They witnessed the outdoor kitchen being demolished by a storm that somehow left the outdoor loo untouched but nearly uprooted the coconut tree, when it pushed its trunk forward and left it crooked. The scene became such a confusing whirl that they could not distinguish one thing from the next. It was so overwhelming; they had to cover their eyes.

It was very clear now why the trees told them to close their eyes whilst being transported through time. Somewhere amidst the confusion, the boys could have sworn they heard Birchard's resonating voice say, 'I see curiosity got the better of you my noble adventurers; once again you failed to listen.'

There was a strange, unidentified flashing light ahead when they landed and Mikal couldn't contain the urge to rush off to investigate, despite Birchard's warning. When he got nearer, it looked like a flashing, green transparent glass with bright stars in the middle. It reminded him of something that he could not recall at the time.

It throbbed and made a subtle, whirring sound when he stroked it. He soon found that his hands were stuck, and were gradually taking on the colour of the glass. As he watched mystified, a light from the stars within it encircled him and drew him through the centre like a magnet with a loud "VOOOOM" that echoed through the air.

'Mikal ... what are you doing? Come back!' Mel yelled, as he ran towards the flashing green light to try to save him.

Similar to Mikal, Mel paid no attention to Birchard when he tried to stop him. His cousin had disappeared into that thingy, and he was going to rescue him. He didn't even bother to touch the shiny, green glass like Mikal; he bravely ran straight through it as the green light encircled him.

It took only a few seconds before another dazzlingly light hit his eyes. This time it was the sunlight streaming down on a sandy beach, with its receding tide and shrubs edging the coastline. His eyes scanned the area in the hot, hazy sunlight, before he saw Mikal looking very bewildered, and ran towards him.

'Why did you follow me Mel?' Mikal asked.

'I wanted to rescue you ...where are we?' Mel replied

'Dunno - haven't got a clue! It looks like we've been transported to another dimension; which could be kinda cool!'

'Another dimension!' Mel shouted. 'Your head must be

in the twilight zone! How could that be "kinda cool" are you stupid or something?'

'Look Mel, I was only trying to suss things out!'

'We've left the magic trees behind. What if something happens, there will be no one to help us. I tell you what; we'd better get back through that ... that ... thingy, before it disappears!' Mel said angrily.

'Just chill Mel, don't worry. You know the trees always come when we're in trouble and call for help.'

'Maybe not this time Mikal ... not this time. I have a strange feeling about this.'

Mikal suddenly stopped listening to Mel's lecture when he heard the sound of the waves splashing against the rocks. It sounded very familiar.

'Uh oh!' he said. 'Mel, I think I'm dreaming again and this time you're in it.'

'What?' I am not dreaming - I am looking right at you. Here, feel this!' Mel leant forward and pinched Mikal's nose in the same way that Birchard had pinched him when they first met.

'Ouch! Why did you do that?'

'You said you were dreaming, and I was in it so I wanted

to wake you up.'

'Don't be silly,' Mikal replied, rubbing the tip of his nose that had suddenly gone red.

He turned to look at the scenery and noticed the sand beneath his trainers. It reminded him of something he had already experienced; a bit like déjà vu. All of a sudden, the pieces of the puzzle fell together; it was the same deserted beach he had seen in his hazy, Jamaican dream that was somewhere in a distant era. He remembered saying he wanted to find it, and had even wished it, but he did not think for one minute that he could.

A moment of anxiety came over him and he called out for the magic trees. Mel gave him a look that said, I told you so; when he had no reply; just before he saw the boats and the strange people. They had dark skin and black drooping hair with hardly any clothes on. *How odd!*

'Do you think we should go to greet them?'

'No, I'm not hanging around here - we need to find our magic trees,' said Mel.

They were suddenly, startled by a rustling sound from the bushes behind and before they could move, four men dressed in a loincloth sprang out of it with pointed spears.

They ran towards them shouting something strange and it was then that the boys realised that they were alarmingly visible once again. They had lost their cloaks, somewhere in between the flashing green light and the beach.

Mikal grabbed Mel's hand and they ran along the beach with the men in full chase. Their speed was no match for these guys. They ran like trained athletes - strong competition for Olympic champions. Mikal really felt he was reliving his dream when one of them grabbed him from behind He struggled to free himself, but the stranger's grip, which was much too strong.

Mel tried to turn back to defend him but Mikal yelled, 'Mel run. Don't turn back, run Mel ... run. Try and find our magic trees.'

Mel ran off again, yanking his trainers out of the thick sand with each step. He looked behind just in time to see Mikal bravely kicked the man firmly in his sacred area and then on his shin. The man hollered and sunk to his knees in excruciating pain.

Freed from his grip, Mikal ran off to catch up with Mel. Through the bushes, they ran like crazed animals, breathing heavily as they raced passed huge, green leaves dampened by the dew; and wild animals that squealed and quickly ran out of their way. *Strange pigs!* Mel thought.

Reaching an area of the island that looked safe, they squatted in between the bushes to catch their breath and check if the men were still in pursuit. They could hear them getting nearer and the boys knew they had to find the energy to keep running.

'Pssst! Pssst!'

'What's that?' Mel whispered.

Mikal pointed to some shrubs behind him. 'It's coming from over there I think.'

They heard the sound again, Pssst! Pssst!'

Mel looked and saw a young boy about his height, peeping out from behind a rock, slightly hidden by the shrubs. The boy wore a skimpy loincloth like the others, with the bit stretched between his legs, embarrassingly hanging loose. His drooping hair rested on his skinny, tanned chest and his eyes flickered with warmth that was much friendlier than that of their chasers.

'Pssst!' Pssst!' he repeated and gestured to them to come over. It seemed like he wanted to help them, but just as they rose up to make a move, strong arms reached out from the bushes and grabbed Mikal. Pulled up from the ground, Mikal was looking straight into the eyes of the strange man he had kicked in self-defence.

'Let me go!' Mikal yelled, kicking his legs and banging his fist against the man's chest.

The man looked at him sternly without flinching or uttering a word. As he struggled, Mikal saw two other men trying to capture Mel, but the young boy grabbed his hand and ran off with him in tow.

Mikal was unsure of the boy's intentions, so he shouted, 'Fight back Mel, fight back!' but there was no time for this.

The boy ran so fast that Mel struggled to keep up with him. He dragged him into a bushy area, which Mel thought looked a bit like the Wendover Hills back home.

'Where are you taking me?' Mel asked the boy.

The boy just looked at Mel and gave him a trusting, smile, which somehow soothed his anxiety. Soon they came to an opening in the side of a hill. He leapt into it with Mel, then crouched and checked to see if they were followed.

When he was sure they were not, he crawled along the narrow path and signalled to Mel to do the same. The path led to a spacious area with a wooden table and sections of the ground covered with green leaves for beds. The fire in the middle was roasting something on a stick and the flickering flames revealed another entrance in the corner.

Two children - younger than the one who led him there, played quietly on the ground, whilst a barefooted woman with hair flopped across her brow tended the roast. She wore a sash stretching from her shoulders to her hips and skimpy clothing that barely covered what it was meant to.

Mel was more concerned about the man sitting near the entrance. He was dressed like the "chasers" with a serious look in his eyes. When he saw Mel appeared behind the boy; he pushed the boy aside, tripped Mel up, and skilfully flipped and positioned his spear to create a barrier between them.

Mel fell to the ground and stayed put, eying the threatening man. However, the boy quickly came to his rescue and said something to the man who then lowered his spear.

Seeing the commotion the woman walked towards the boy, pulled his ear and spoke to him firmly, as if she was telling him off. Afterwards, he signalled to Mel to walk over to the fire. Mel moved cautiously to where they stood, and now it was the woman's turn.

She looked him up and down, examining his clothes and making funny sounds as if she disapproved. Then she ushered him to the table, handed him a plate of fruits and signalled to him firmly to eat, under the watchful eye of the guard. One false move and goodness knows what he would do.

Mel glanced between him and the thing roasting on the fire and for a moment pictured himself replacing it. Realising shortly after that he was not in the company of cannibals, Mel decided to find out who they were, and why they lived in a hillside cave rather than a house or tent, but he wasn't sure how to do this. Then he had an idea.

Standing in front of the boy, he patted his chest like Tarzan. 'Me, Mel,' he said proudly. He then touched the boy's chest and asked, 'What's your name?'

The boy stepped back and looked at him strangely. Mel patted his chest again and repeated, 'Me ... Mel...what's your name?' This time, the boy smiled - he understood - *thank goodness!*

'Teeka,' he replied. He patted his chest like Mel and said it again, 'Teeka.'

Mel smiled. 'Thank you for rescuing me,' he said. 'But I need to find my cousin. He was caught in the woods, or, maybe it was a forest - we were separated.'

Teeka did not understand so using a piece of twig from the ground Mel drew a stick image of Mikal being, held near a bush by a man. Teeka's face lit up again

'Yah! Yah!' he said, nodding his head, which to Mel meant that once again he understood.

Teeka said something to his mum. She listened and then nodded. Seconds later, he took Mel's hand and led him out of the cave through the other entrance, at a much slower pace than before. Arriving at the spot where they had last seen Mikal, they searched all around, calling out his name, but there was no sign of him.

After a few attempts they heard muffled sounds and found Mikal tied up on the ground behind a bush. None of the natives was around, so Teeka used the sharp flint knife, concealed within his loincloth to cut him loose.

Mikal felt uneasy by Teeka's presence at first, especially when he pulled out the blade, but when he untied him, Mikal realised that he really wanted to help them.

'Mel I'm so glad you found me, I was worried about you.

Where did you run off to with this boy from the woods?'

'This is Teeka; he saved me from the men who were chasing us and took me to his home. He came back with me to find you.'

'How did you find out his name, does he speak English?'

'No, I used Tarzan language and Art,' replied Mel. The conversation stopped abruptly when they heard shouting - their chasers were returning!

The boys were on the run again along the beach. If the men caught them this time, they knew they would never get away. Teeka watched the chase feeling very helpless. He had just decided to fetch the chief, when suddenly the ground started to rumble and shake.

The chasers and the rest of the natives who ran out from the bushes, staggered and swayed uncontrollably as they tried to balance themselves.

Mel and Mikal were very alarmed when the earth shook to such an extent that a gaping hole split the ground; creating a division between where they stood and the rest of the people When the tremors stopped just as suddenly as they began, the natives watched anxiously, anticipating another flare up.

Then unexpectedly, something strange took place. An alarming sound came from the huge, split in the ground. It sounded as if something was being, forced out. The natives moved back towards the bushes, looking fearfully to see what monstrous thing would emerge.

When Mel and Mikal peered cautiously into the opening, two unidentified forms were painstakingly making their way upwards, screeching like faulty car brakes. They looked around for somewhere to hide; anticipating the worst, but before they could, two scorched heads slowly emerged from the hole.

It took a while for the boys to realise that it was their magic trees, who had ditched their invisibility. Rising from the hole, the magic trees levitated above the split ground like fearless gods, lifted by unseen forces.

There was a hush amongst the stunned natives, who stared at them with opened mouths. Then slowly, one by one, they knelt down and started chanting something strange but yet fascinating, 'Ohommmmm, Ohommmmm.'

The trees suspended themselves in the air with arms folded and feet together, lapping up the adoration as they waited for the worshiping to stop. Then they surprisingly bowed their heads and calmly said to the boys, 'Did you call, oh masters?'

'Masters! What are they doing?' Mel whispered to Mikal. 'They are not genies or gods.'

'I think it's a trick, but let's just play along with it. At least we know now, how they levitated over our Grandparents' garden fence.'

Mikal thought the trees might have found their lost capes, so he shouted, 'Make us invisible,' for all the natives to hear, even if they did not understand. Birchard stepped forward, bowed and covered them with their capes.

The natives gasped when the boys instantly disappeared before their eyes. They had never seen anything like this. In awe, they started bowing and chanting that "Ohomining" thing all over again.

'Where did you guys disappear to? Did you know, four crazy men in their nappies, carrying spears chased us and one of them kidnapped me? A native boy rescued Mel and took him to his hillside cave without a view, and, and…,'

'Whoa! Wait a minute Mikal,' said Birchard. 'We're the Gods here - you two ran off remember!'

'Listen guys, I'm not sure what happened why we lost

you. It might have been an unexpected glitch in our time travelling compass.'

'A glitch!' said Mikal. 'I think you're pulling our legs, Elmstead - don't you think so Mel?'

'Yep, I think so too. I can see it in their faces.'

'The truth is guys, we wanted you to have a bit of an adventure without us hanging around,' said Birchard. 'And from what we can see, you got it. However, we didn't plan to abandon you. You came to this deserted beach that is certainly fully occupied now, through the same vortex we normally use in disguise.'

'So that's what it was - the tunnel vortex! I knew it looked familiar,' said Mikal.

'We followed you through the vortex, but accidentally ended up inside the core of the island. Did you guys know that there's an inner sun down there?' said Elmstead.

'Down where?'

'In the earth's core!'

'What! Nah, can't be ...that's impossible!'

'Yes there is Mikal.'

Whilst the natives continued "Ohomining" Both trees waved their branch hands and conjured up captivating, visual images of a sun, in the island's core and the sweltering, ground beneath it.

'The sun looked real and it was extremely hot; our cooling mechanism couldn't cope. It scorched our trunks and, almost set alight our branches,' said Elmstead. 'We had to create a "man-made"...sorry; I meant a "tree-made" earthquake to get out and somehow managed to save your capes.'

'Were you two hurt?'

'We are fine Mel, no need to fuss!' said Birchard as the visual images faded.

'Wow ... amazing! One day I might find my way there; but I'll just make sure I have a fireman's outfit and hose first.'

'Did you boys have any idea who your chasers are? They are the Arawaks or Tainos - the first settlers in Jamaica that we told you about?'

'No,' we didn't know that,' said Mel.

'Mikal ... you've seen them before, haven't you?'

'What! Mikal you know these guys?'

'Yeah ... I met them in my dreams.'

'Met them in your what?'

'We are sorry Mikal, but I guess it's time we revealed that we were responsible for your dream encounter too.'

'I knew it - I was right! But how did you ...?'

'Ah, stop right there! We won't give away our secret, but let's just say in time you will figure it out.'

'You bet! Mikal replied. 'And when I do, I will let you know about it.'

Birchard smiled and said, 'No doubt you will.'

'You know I think those peaceful Tainos or Arawaks chased you, because they thought you'd attack them first, and take away their newly, found land,' said Elmstead.

'Peaceful Arawaks ... are you kidding!' said Mikal. 'I think I've heard it all now -can we go now please.'

'Wait! I want to say goodbye to Teeka, the boy, who rescued me.'

The natives gasped when the boys became visible again, by what they thought were the l powers of these tree gods.

Teeka had waited patiently for them to return to visibility; he was impressed, but not astonished like the others. They all embraced, and he gave Mel a small stone drawing of himself.

'Goodbye Teeka, thanks for everything.' Teeka smiled

and bowed 'Maybe we will meet again someday,' said Mel.

'Not if those chasers are still here,' said Mikal.

Before leaving, the magic trees greeted the bewildered Chief, who appeared in a fabulous headdress and a well-fitted loincloth. Poor soul, he had missed all the excitement!

The trees used levitation to return the displaced rocks to their origin, and created another rumble in the ground to repair the crack.

'You know what Mel; I think those ancient Egyptians used levitation to lift the stones that made the pyramids. I wonder who taught them that!'

'Trust you to think of something like that. Maybe we should ask Grandpa Dee - he will know the answer.'

The natives cheered as the boys and their magic trees entered the brightly lit vortex; and the sight of the glowing, vortex, left Teeka wishing that he had the power to take off with them.

'Be careful what you wish for,' Elmstead whispered to him through the wind, in that strange, native language.

*E*lmstead re-programmed their time travel compass for another era, but when they landed, once again they didn't recognise the place. It certainly wasn't the deserted beach they had just left behind, or the peaceful village of Rock Spring.

Instead of sunny blue skies, there were heavy grey clouds, and there was something wrong with the atmosphere. They were swaying uncontrollably, much worse than in the earthquake on the deserted beach, and could hardly balance themselves.

Mel suddenly realised that he was facing his biggest fear, 'STRONG WINDS" he shouted.

'It's more like a hurricane,' Birchard yelled back. 'We've landed right in the middle of Hurricane Gilbert that devastated Jamaica in 1988.'

'How did we end up here?'

'I am not sure, we were supposed to land in Montego Bay in 1965, but instead we've landed in 1988. Perhaps there was a glitch in the ether that affected my equipment,' said Elmstead.

'Oh that's just great! Are you sure that this is not another one of your tricks?'

'Seriously Mikal, this isn't a trick. There is a problem with my inbuilt navigator. Maybe being in the earth's core over heated it. Or, maybe you boys weren't focusing on the era we wanted to get to, during the time travel from the village to the deserted beach.'

'What! It's not our fault that we ended up ...'

Mikal stopped abruptly, as he remembered that they had indeed been watching the trees activate the time travelling compass in the village; and in the excitement, forgot to focus on the time period after they left the deserted beach.

The rain pelted down so heavily that within minutes, they were all absolutely, soaked and the monstrous winds felt a thousand times stronger than what Mel experienced in his grandparents' garden.

The winds roared fiercely above their heads, pushing and almost pulling them off their branch seats like a strong force. The magic trees plucked them out of their branch seats and placed them in between themselves and a lamppost.

Clinging to the lamp post the boys, who had never in their dreams experienced anything like this, watched in horror through windswept eyes, as parked cars yanked from the ground like light metal; and roofs ripped off from house tops, by the torrent winds, slammed into other things.

'Hold on tight!' yelled Birchard. 'The winds are blowing at nearly 150 miles per hour; destroying everything in its path.'

The trees desperately tried to re-activate the navigator and were struggling to keep grounded; whilst the winds forcefully tore through their branches, making them sway in all directions.

'Try your navigator again,' Birchard said to Elmstead. 'We've got to get the boys out of here before the hammering winds, sweeping through our branches topple us.'

The swirling wheel of clouds immediately above them carried the force of the turbulent winds that were totally wrecking the area. Mel and Mikal noticed that the clouds spiralled out of a huge spot in the middle that reminded them of an eye.

The only difference was that it looked gigantic, to put it mildly, and didn't blink as it moved along, getting a bird's eye view of the whole island beneath it.

Compared to the spiralling clouds with the horrendous winds moving anticlockwise around it, the eye appeared to be completely calm and still. Except, for one horrifying moment, when Mel and Mikal imagined that it had an extremely wide mouth, mocking their predicament.

The vision made them lose their grip on the lamppost, just as a swirl of raging winds, unexpectedly tore around the corner, and whipped them up in the air like ragdolls, out of the grasp of their magic trees.

They somersaulted helplessly in the clutches of the powerful, roaring winds, circulating menacingly all around them. It battered their faces, pulled them further upwards and made them feel like they were having the life sucked out of them.

The thought of being caught up in that powerful mass, swirling around the still, hollow eye and mocking circular mouth, high above them was their biggest fear. That hollow space was something they definitely didn't want to explore.

Hanging onto the pole, with their bodies outstretched on either side and flapping in the wind like flags, was their only security in the open skies.

The fact that they were firmly, secured in the ground had so far, prevented Elmstead and Birchard from being uprooted by the turbulent winds. Now they had to think of a way to rescue the boys.

Birchard who had always been the more courageous of the two, released his roots from the ground and with a quick levitating leap, he ascended high in the air like a spring against the force of the violent winds.

He managed to steady himself long enough to grab the boys and descended to the ground as quickly as he ascended, against the force of the winds.

Within seconds after Birchard's touchdown, Elmstead at last managed to re-activate his navigator. They instantly formed a circle and in the blink of an eye were miraculously, ejected into another era, leaving the turbulent devastation behind.

They landed in Montego Bay, in an atmosphere that was quite sunny and calm in comparison to the scene they had just left behind.

They were in a gully, otherwise known as a ravine, with steps leading to the road above called Perry Street. The trees shook their drenched leaves, showering raindrops all over them.

'Why is it called a gully or a ravine?' asked Mikal.

'Because it's an area worn out by many years of flooding,' Elmstead explained. 'I'm sure you both remember your Grandma's stories about the flash floods in the gully that swept cars out to sea. The flood rose so high that, at times she couldn't walk home from school.'

Walking ahead of the trees along the pebbled path, they could see shops and small houses on either side supported by wooden stilts.

NO TRESPASSING

At the top of the gully, opposite the worn out steps, the path led to an interesting narrow gap, covered with moss. Mikal squeezed through to see what was beyond it and Mel followed, pleading with him to turn back.

'You always go off to explore things and get us into trouble Mikal, just like what happened with the green vortex and the stream - you know - the one that turned into a river.'

'Don't worry Mel, this is different. It will be ok this time, trust me!'

The narrow gap opened up into a wider path that the boys followed until they came to a dead end, and at this point Mel really wanted to turn back.

'What's that over there? It looks like another opening. Can you see it?'

'Yes, but I can also see a sign that says "No Trespassing" Mikal, so let's obey and turn back.'

'Come on Mel, let's just have a peek, it won't do any

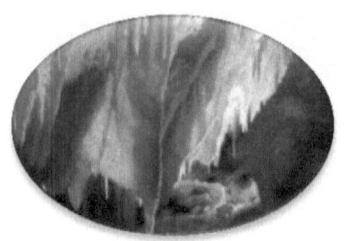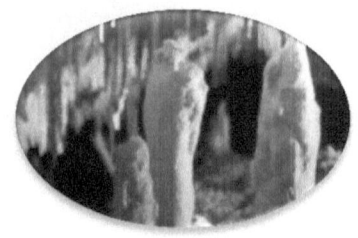

harm.' Mel eventually gave in, and Mikal reached for his hand to pull him closer as they crunched their way noisily along the gravelled path.

'Shush, walk quietly. Someone might hear us.'

'Don't be silly Mel ... there is no one around.'

The mysterious opening looked like an entrance to a cave. Mel only wanted to have a peek from the outside, but as Mikal felt intrigued by the thought of what could possibly be on the inside, he reluctantly decided to follow. *Someone had to make sure that he came out safe for heaven's sake!*

The boys cautiously entered the unlit entrance and moved further and further into the cave, until they arrived at another opening lower than the first and crawled through. They found themselves in a section of the cave with a much higher ceiling that was very quiet except for the sound of dripping water into the murky pool below.

A beam of sunlight streamed in from a hole above, illuminating a section of the walls that were breathtakingly beautiful. The walls shone like gold from years of saturation by seeping chemicals, like iron and potassium nitrate.

Mel wished they had a camera to capture the fascinating images and Mikal wondered how long it would have taken to form this amazing scene. They would have been amazed to know that the cave was 35 million years old.

Although fascinated by the beauty of the cave, its eerie silence and the slow dripping water, gave Mel the creeps. 'I think we should go now Mikal, this place feels weird.'

'You're always scared; you should try to be brave like me.'

'Oh yeah ... you mean like when you were scared of the tiny lizard that jumped on your back.'

'I wasn't really scared then Mel, I was just pretending.'

'Just pretending! Ok, what about the crocodile and the hurricane - weren't you scared then?' Something distracted Mikal before he could respond.

'Shush Mel! I think I saw something move.'

'Where?'

'Up there ... in that corner to your right. Maybe we were making too much noise and woke something up.'

'Something like what?' said Mel.

'I don't know ... I've never been in a cave before.

'What type of things do you find in a cave apart from those things hanging down and sticking up?'

'You mean those stalactites and stalagmites, how about insects and monsters.'

'Oh stop it Mikal! I think you're scared too.'

Over in the corner, something moved again and this time they both heard it quite clearly.

'What do you think that was?'

'I don't know, you should have turned back like I said.'

Mikal ignored Mel's comment and started looking for a way out. The sunbeam had disappeared and except for a few low rocks, there was nowhere visible to hide. They heard fluttering sounds and suddenly a number of squeaking things with flapping wings, rose from above the rocks, filling the air in droves and squeaking louder as they flew towards them.

'They are bats ... hundreds of them!' Mel yelled.

The bats flew above and around their heads, emitting a dreadful, squeaky, clicking sound, whilst the boys repeatedly swung their arms above their heads to fend them off. Some flew off, but many more rose from their slumber and began to encircle them. They were going to have to find a way out!

They were in luck. The sunbeam filtered through the crack above them again, revealing a path that was not visible before, and they ran towards it, unsure of where it would lead. However, the furious bats disturbed from their slumber, were hot on their heels - hell bent on chasing them out of their dwellings.

They ran through the winding path and came to a dead end on the edge of a ledge. The ledge led to nowhere apart from a rocky trail thirty feet below, with a trickling stream making its way between the embedded rocks.

They were glad to see light, but Mel had an overwhelming feeling of despair that he could not ignore. It was the end of the line, and the sound of the squeaking bats closing in was deafening.

'We're trapped! What are we gonna do?'

The vines hanging from some of the trees close by gave him an idea. They hung a few metres above a sturdy looking tree, conveniently positioned beneath the ledge.

'We can't turn back now Mel, so we're going to have to reach for those vines over there, and use them to slide down unto that tree directly below.'

'What tree?'

Mikal pointed to it. 'It's a long way down, but we can do it, and hopefully get back to our magic trees.'

'What's the alternative?' Mel asked.

'To go back the way we came and meet those horrid creatures full on. They will probably fly all over our heads, squeaking in our ears and who knows ... they could bite us!'

'Ok that does it ...come on let's jump,' said Mel.

'Hold on, I'll go and get the vines first and then swing back onto the ledge to pick you up - got it?'

'Yep, just hurry before the bats catch up with us. And, be careful ... I wouldn't want you to miss your landing,' Mel joked, even though he was scared stiff.

Mikal aimed, jumped, and caught hold of a vine and then another as planned. He swung back towards the ledge; steadying the vines, as he got nearer, so that Mel could jump on as agreed.

Meanwhile he could hear Mel yelling for him to hurry, as the bats were approaching the ledge, but luckily, for him, the glaring sunlight confused them. They backed away from the ledge, circled the air clicking and squeaking, and seconds later flew back to their resting place. *Phew!*

With the bats out of the way, Mel jumped onto the vine and both vines swung back into position right above the targeted tree. Carefully they slid down inch by inch, until they were close enough to get ready to jump onto its branches.

Mikal was clearly taking charge of the mission, but to Mel this was like "Mission Impossible" out in the jungle and he knew he needed to be brave to see it through.

'Ready Mel? Ok three, two, one, here we go!'

'Aaarrgh! Aaarrgh!' Their drawn out yells echoed in the silence until they landed on the branches of the targeted tree.

'Oh my gosh, we made it! I thought my heart was going to leap out of my chest when we jumped.'

'Me too Mel, but it was either that or face those bats. I didn't realise that you had so much courage.'

'Thanks. I'm glad this tree is here, because Birchard and Elmstead might not have heard our call for help.'

Exhausted from their "running jump", they rested their heads on the comfy branch, thinking of a way to get down.

A few minutes later a sound that made them jump,

interrupted their temporary rest.

'Ahem!'

'Mel did you cough?'

'No, I thought you did.'

'So, who was that then?'

Mel shrugged his shoulders, 'Dunno!'

He mimicked a cough and waited quietly for the sound to repeat but nothing happened. Then they noticed that the tree, seemed to be swaying, *or, was it moving* they pondered. It took them a while to realise that unbelievably, it was trudging along slowly through the rich vegetation.

'Mikal what's going on? I thought our magic trees were the only trees that could do this type of thing.'

'I don't know any more than you do, so ask the tree.'

'I don't think it can talk. Something weird is going on here. We need to get down from this tree right now,' Mel said angrily and banged his fist on the branch. 'I really wish Birchard or Elmstead were here to help us.'

A startling voice surprisingly rang out in the still air from below. 'Did you guys call ... again?'

'Who said that? Elmstead, is that you?' asked the boys.

'NOPE!' the voice replied loudly, in a tone bordering

between that of a male and female.

'What! Then who are you?' the boys asked.

'Who am I? You guys are making a habit of calling for your magic trees to rescue you, don't you think? The crocodile the stream and now this cave!' The voice replied, ending the sentence with a cough and a soft feminine squeak. The voice then switched to a masculine tone.

'Don't you boys ever learn? I must say though, using the Leaping Vines showed good initiative; I didn't think you had it in you!'

'What do you mean,' Mikal asked. 'Do you know us and our magic trees? And, how do you know about our calls for help?'

'Oh yes! I know you both and your magic trees. I am their Godlink. I see and report on all things that they do.'

'What's a Godlink?' the boys asked.

'Godlink or Seers as we are also known, run things in Treeland, because we're full of wisdom to take charge,' the voice said proudly. 'A bit like your Grandpa Dee.'

The boys felt confused. They pictured Grandpa Dee taking charge of things and quickly dismissed it. Grandma Cee would not allow it, and being a Grandpa just didn't sound the same as being a Godlink. What does that really mean?

'Why can't we see your face?' Mel asked.

'Good question. It is to do with respect. Godlinks never reveal themselves fully to youngsters.'

'Godlink ... Seer ... do you have another name?'

'Those are my job titles Mel,' The Seer replied, as he trudged along. 'I don't mind being called either, but my real name is Goodwin. Don't know why I am called that, because physically, I am really a sturdy oak tree. Why didn't they name me Oakley! That's more appropriate, don't you think?'

'Well, yes... I guess so,' said Mel. 'But you could consider changing it by Deed Poll.'

'What!' The Seer shrieked. 'Are you crazy? My "Deeds" don't get altered on Polls!'

'Sorry ... just a suggestion! We will call you "The Seer" if you don't mind,' said Mel.

'Where are you taking us?'

'That's obvious isn't it Mikal - you're being kidnapped!'

'KIDNAPPED ... PUT US DOWN RIGHT NOW!'

'Calm down guys... just kidding! I am taking you back to

your temporary guardians! What did you think?'

'Oh! Phew ... what a relief!' they both exclaimed.

'Sorry for the trouble, we just wanted to look into the cave; but then we got chased by bats and couldn't find a way out.'

'Chased by bats ... do you mean Ratbats Mel? That is what Jamaicans call them. Did they bite you?'

'No,' Mel replied, looking wide-eyed as he recalled the scene. 'They just flew over our heads and chased us out.'

'They chased you out! Hahaha! Just like the Green Monkeys ... serves you right!'

'You knew about that?'

'Yes, I was looking on ... from a distance mind you! As the "All Seeing Eye" I can see everything you do. By the way, that cave is not safe you know. Strictly speaking, it is supposed to be, closed to the public; that is why there was a "No Trespassing" sign. I don't mean to be rude, but ... can't you guys read?'

'I told him, but he wouldn't listen,' said Mel.

'Luckily my intuition and navigation came in handy. Next time, you may not be so fortunate to be, rescued by a Godlink such as myself. Anyway, thought I would mention that another glitch in Elmstead's navigator led to you ending up in the wrong year again. That is why you found the cave. It was completely hidden in your Grandma's time.'

'I'm glad we did - it was awesome! Those stalactites and stalagmites were amazing,' said Mikal.

'Indeed. Calcium Carbonate in seeping water droplets helped to formed them. Did you know this island and cave you've been traipsing through, once sat beneath the Pacific Ocean?'

'No ... how long ago was that?' asked Mel.

'About 115 million years ago.'

'115 million years! You're talking dinosaur times.'

'That is awesome ... legendary!' said Mikal.

'Legendary?' said The Seer

'Oh that's just a new phrase my school friends and I use.'

'I see,' the Seer replied, looking very puzzled.

'How did the cave form in that gigantic ocean?'

'Ah ... that's a tale for another chapter Mel. Come with me!'

❧Chapter 28: The Amazing Crystal Ball❧

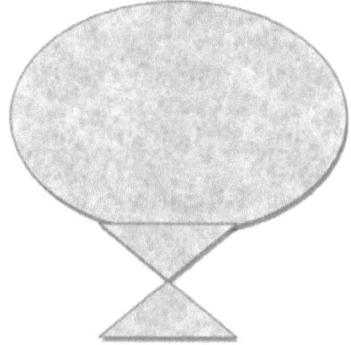

The Seer was in the open doing some sort of meditation with his eyes closed. He wore a hood that partly covered his face and made him look like a monk.

'Look at that Mel, who'd have thought Birchard and Elmstead would have a Godlink with a hoodie.'

'Oh yeah! Thought he said he was a "Seer"- how can he see with his eyes closed.'

The Seer waved his leafy arms at the scenery full of trees and plants as if he was Moses parting the red sea. A rumbling sound filled the air and long strips of tree vines; like those, they had leapt onto earlier, to escape from the Ratbats, swung into position.

As if commanded by a hidden power, the vines slotted together, to form a huge curtain. There was a sudden stillness in the air. The wind ceased; the birds stopped chirping and the leaves on the surrounding trees hung perfectly still.

'What's happening?' the puzzled boys asked.

'It's time for the next chapter,' The Seer replied. 'Wait just one minute,' he said fumbling inside his trunk just like their magic trees. He pulled out helmets with face screens that fitted neatly below the chin; goggles, gloves and black, stretchy outfits, similar to the "onesies" they wore to bed.

'Here, put these on and take off your capes; you won't need those for a while,' he grinned, showing off his lopsided twig-teeth. 'Now, just step right through into the next chapter; it's in fast track 3D!'

'Won't we need some 3D specs?'

'No, but the helmets and goggles will come in handy Mel.' The vine curtains parted with unseen hands, ushering Mel and Mikal through, and to their amazement, an enormous blue crystal ball stood in front of them.

It flickered on and off, clocking up scenery speeds, covering thousands or millions of years at a time. As they stood mesmerised, the crystal ball changed colour and a huge piece of land with a thick mist above it appeared.

'This is Jamaica in its infancy,' said The Seer. 'Millions of

years after it rose from the Pacific Ocean on a molten rock, now called the Caribbean Plate, and slowly drifted to where it is now.'

'Oh my days - you're kidding! Are we going to be watching Jamaica coming into being in the woods like a movie?'

'That's right Mel, except it is real - not science fiction.'

With eyes glued onto the crystal ball, they watched the scenery changing at fast-forward speeds; the mist lifted and centuries later, vegetation sprung up over its surface. Absolutely fascinated, the boys wanted to be right in the midst of the crystal ball, experiencing the changes and surprisingly, The Seer permitted this.'

'To go inside shout "Enter Now" and step in,' he said. 'Enter now,' they both shouted.

The crystal ball wobbled and the scene amazingly stretched outwards, wrapping itself around them as they stepped in. The speed of events slowed down once they were on the inside; allowing them to touch the variety of rare, fascinating plants with their gloves on; some of which were extinct in their own time.

Being in an atmosphere millions of years before their time was absolutely, fantastic. On the sea front, they saw weird stones and pebbles with the remains of tiny, encrusted sea creatures. *Yuck how gross!*

The boys were surprised when a slit in the earth, suddenly appeared near their feet. It slowly stretched along the length of the ground, as if it was unzipping to show off its strange interior. As it widened, steam flew out in all directions.

They weren't sure how, but quite unexpectedly, the boys found themselves being pulled right inside of it. Their helmets automatically fastened as some strange force, dragged them into the core of the island.

They were slipping and sliding at quite a speed. Rocks of all colours sped by; some looked like marble, or black like coal, some were green, reddish and others even sparkled like gold. They gripped and quickly let go off rocks that were red hot to the touch, even with their gloves on.

The heat increased the deeper they slid, 'Oh my god, it's

really hot down here,' Mikal yelled. 'I think we really need that fireman outfit and hose you mentioned earlier to survive this.'

Surprisingly, the helmet protected their heads and faces and the stretchy outfits prevented their body from being scorched. Sliding at such a fast pace the boys did not have time to think of how they were going to get back, but as it grew hotter by the minute, they knew they had to get out.

As if he had read their thoughts, the boys heard the Seer's voice in stereo saying, 'Shout, "Out now" to be on the outside.'

Without hesitating they shouted, 'Out Now!'

The Seer immediately transported them back to where he stood, absolutely drenched in sweat and in need of a drink.

The "showroom crack" sealed up once they were out, but shortly after a loud explosion filled the air; throwing them off balance even though they were on the outside. Through the crystal ball, they could see and hear a volcanic explosion in the ocean, and on the horizon, something seemed to be rising higher and higher.

Oh … my…gosh, look!' Mel shouted.

'An enormous mountain of water, higher than a skyscraper and almost as wide as the width of the ocean, rushed at full force towards the land. At the sight of it, the boys couldn't help screaming; partly from being alarmed, but also from the excitement.

'Don't worry, the Tsunami can't harm you,' said The Seer. 'Remember ... you're an outside observer.'

The ocean rose and buried the land with such force that only water was visible in the crystal ball; the island had totally disappeared. When it reappeared, it was in the depths of the ocean, covered with sea organisms and limestone that were seeping through the surface and creating holes.

Mel and Mikal watched as the holes sunk deeper into the land, stretching wider and wider. By the time it took the crystal ball to register a few more million years, the erosion had formed into caves of all different shapes and sizes.

This scene was much too exciting just to watch, so Mikal suddenly shouted 'Enter now!' With his goggles in place, Mikal stepped right through the crystal ball onto the island on the ocean floor, to observe this amazing sight, passing right before his very eyes.

But, to his horror, surprisingly another explosion occurred that tossed him some metres along the ocean bed that was beginning to rock and shift.

'Mikal ... you fool, get out now!' Mel yelled.

'Out now,' Mikal shouted, just before the shifting, volcanic movement tossed him outside the crystal ball. Looking back, he had just enough time to see the island rising as a huge land mass from the ocean bed, to the surface.

When the crystal ball finally showed the Blue Mountain peak, they knew it was all over. Another ten million years went by before Jamaica had fully resurfaced. It had conquered the ocean and was now back, in full swing: a bit bald from lack of vegetation, but plenty of hardened limestone to endure the test of time.

'Woooow that was fantastic! An amazing 3D film ... the best history lesson ever!' they both exclaimed.

'I'm glad you liked it!' The Seer replied.

'I wonder if Jamaica will ever sink again.'

'I hope not Mel, because sadly, it would be like the "Port Royal" catastrophe all over again.'

The Seer clicked his fingers and the vine curtains and crystal ball all disappeared without a trace. 'Come; let's get back to Birchard and Elmstead. I left them flirting with a cute little tree earlier.'

On their way back, Mel could not get the sight of the rising Blue Mountain peak out of his mind.

'I don't know about going back into a cave Mr Seer, but one day I'm gonna climb that famous Blue Mountain.'

'Now that's the spirit Mel - I knew you had it in you.'

The Seer led them back to the magic trees and disappeared after they thanked him.

'He will probably be looking down on us with his "All seeing eye" like he told us,' said Mel.

They both gasped as The Seer's voice responded in the wind, 'Yes, I'll be "seeing" you my little adventurers. Treerio!'

Elmstead and Birchard were deep in conversation with the cute tree, so the boys didn't bother to mention the meeting with their Godlink - they would find out eventually.

'Oh there you are,' said Elmstead, 'I was beginning to wonder where you had disappeared to. Let me introduce you to the lovely Alma - isn't she beautifully green!'

Alma did not have face, arms and legs like their magic trees, but she was the cutest tree they had ever seen. Somehow, she extended a leafy branch with fruits attached to the boys, and surprisingly said, 'Hello, how are you both today? It's really nice to meet you.'

The boys weren't sure what part of her the voice came from, but they both politely said, 'It's very nice to meet you too Alma.'

'Would you like to try these,' she said, handing them some of her fruits. 'They taste good!' The boys ate what they could only presume was a small, oval fruit with a hard kernel underneath. It was sweet but not as delicious as the mangoes they had eaten earlier - nothing topped that!

When with some effort they cracked open the core with a stone as instructed; it revealed a sweet inner brown nut that they liked. 'Hmmm ... wait a minute ... it's an almond!' said Mel. 'We didn't know it grew like this.'

'Maybe we should transport Alma to our Grandparents' garden; we would get fresh almonds, and Elmstead would have a new wife,' said Mikal.

'Hahaha, a new wife - didn't know he had one in the first place,' responded Mel.

❧Chapter 30: The Runaway Horse❧

The problem with the time travel compass was at last sorted. They said goodbye to Alma and were all transported safely at last to 1965.

They heard voices as they walked once again along the length of the pebbled gully path. A group of children including young Grandma Cee in her neatly pressed, navy and white school uniform chatted as they walked towards them.

The boys were listening to their chatter, when suddenly, another sound distracted them, and before they knew it, a huge horse came darting round the corner at great speed without a rider.

'It's a runawey harse, get outa de way quick,' the children yelled.

They ran as fast as their legs could carry them towards the steps, extending to Perry Street above. However, instead of running straight ahead, the horse started a mad chase after the children, frothing and panting heavily.

The travelling party stood back to observe the scene. Young Grandma Cee screamed and ran as fast as she could, some distance behind the others, who quickly mounted the steps, two at a time.

With the horse only a few feet away, she tried hard to increase her speed, which was quite a pitiful sight to watch. Somehow she leapt onto the first step and managed to scramble onto the second out of its reach; narrowly missing being nudged by its bridled mouth.

Relieved and in tears, she ran all the way to the top of the winding steps, calling out to the others, who by now had reached the safety of the street above. She watched as the horse galloped off at great speed.

Some minutes later, Mel and Mikal noticed a man running towards them, looking anxious as if he was chasing after something.

'Hexcuse me Sar' he said to another man walking by. 'Yuh see a harse run pass ere?'

'No!' The man replied shaking his head. 'Yuh las yuh harse?'

'Yes, im jus gallop off after mi drap off im back and

nearly bruk me neck.'

'Sarry Sar,' the other man said, 'but me neva see im. Ope yuh find im soon.'

The first man nodded with a worried look on his face. 'Mi ope suh too,' he replied, and running off to continue his search, he shouted back, 'Odda wise mi will lose de bet!'

Mel and Mikal thought this scene was hilarious and were literally shaking with laughter.

"Did you see that Mikal? He will never catch that horse - it shot through that gully like Usain Bolt.'

'Maybe it's a race horse Mel ... the one they call "Long Shot". Hahaha!'

Chapter 31: The Fire Cracker

Ascending from the Gully, they walked along the adjoining road and soon arrived at Perry Street that ran alongside Montego Bay High School.

The residents were getting ready to celebrate the 1962 Jamaican Independence Anniversary; making new outfits, cooking and baking to create a feast.

They found Grandma Cee's house at the top of the street, where she lived with her Great Aunt Rubena - a dressmaker - whom they had met before, and her Uncle Gideon - a local postman. A huge tree stood at the front of the yard that had an outdoor kitchen and icebox, but there were no signs of an outdoor loo.

Recovered from her galloping escapade, she was once again playing outdoors in a frilly red polka dot dress, this time with her friends from next door - Sonia, Teddy and Nully. She kept scanning the end of the road as if she was expecting someone, and it soon became evident that she was looking for her uncle. When he arrived, he gave her gifts - mint balls and Cola that she gulped down.

'Hey wait a minute! Thought she told us not to drink that stuff!' said Mel.

Uncle Gideon unknowingly dropped a handkerchief with his engraved "GM" initials when he hugged her. Mel rescued the handkerchief before her Uncle detected it, along with an abandoned doll that he thought belonged to Grandma Cee.

Shortly after her uncle's arrival, the boys saw Grandma Cee picked up something from a container on the steps of the house. She ran off looking quite pleased with herself and stuffed it in her mouth.

Suddenly they heard a sound like a small explosion, and the smile on her face quickly faded. To their horror, Grandma Cee stood there looking dazed, with wisps of smoke flowing out of her mouth and nose.

First on the scene was her cousin Artwell. A few seconds later, her Uncle Gideon came rushing out; followed by Aunt Rubena and their dog Pupsy.

'What happened,' said her uncle.

'What's dat noise?' Aunt Rubena asked, with cigarette in hand and a dressmaker's tape measure hanging around her neck.

Artwell explained that Grandma Cee had chewed on a small firecracker that resembled a sweet and it went off in her mouth.

'Lawd ave mercy,' said Aunt Rubena. 'What's wrong wid yuh chile? Dat was for de independence celebration. Yuh want fe kill yuhself? Lawd ge mi strent! Yuh going to ave a smoking edache tonight!'

Young Grandma Cee was too shocked to speak. She needed to see a doctor quickly and they all accompanied her.

'Yuh tink she'll be alright?' her Uncle Gideon asked the doctor.

'Yes, she will be fine, but will most likely have a headache for a few days,' the doctor replied.

After they returned to Perry Street, it was time for the magic trees and the boys to leave. The boys asked to stay behind to make sure Grandma Cee was ok; after all, she nearly blew herself up!

'You already know the outcome,' said Birchard. 'Apart

from an occasionally earache, she was fine when you left home. You cannot do anything about it, just like the incident with the horse. So, whisper goodbye, tell her you will see her later - much later in fact - and let's go!'

When they returned to their grandparents' garden, Elmstead gave Mel the plantain and mangoes he had placed inside his trunk.

'Just a few more "souvenirs" to add to those tucked up your shirt. They'll stir up memories for your Grandma.' Mel didn't realise that he had noticed.

'Guess what,' he said. 'Grandma is writing a children's book.'

'A book did you say?' There was a puzzled look on Elmstead's face as he paused, and then said 'That's great, why don't you both have another peek, you might just get an interesting surprise.'

'See you tomorrow same time, same place! Treerio,' they both said, before disappearing in a flash of light similar to the vortex.

Grandma Cee took one look at the boys entering the dining room and cringed.

'Oh look at that mess. Where have you boys been? Timbuktu!'

'Timbuk who?'

'Both of you go and get washed up for lunch right now,' she said sternly. 'You will be scrubbing those T-shirts later!'

Mikal stared at her for a moment. 'I wonder what happen to that cute, happy "smoking" girl we left behind in 1965!' he said to Mel.

They both laughed when Mel replied, 'I guess she's gone to find another firecracker!'

'Mel you know that Timbuktu place Grandma just mentioned; dad told me it was near the river Niger, in the

Sahara, and that it was once a very rich and civilised African city.'

'Really! I thought it was some weird place,' replied Mel. 'Maybe one day we'll go there by a strange, mysterious glitch. Hahaha!'

The phone rang and as Grandma Cee answered it, Mel discreetly placed the souvenirs and mangoes where she could find them. Sometime after the telephone conversation with her cousin Barry; now living in the USA, Grandma Cee spotted them. 'Dee, did you buy these mangoes and plantain?'

'No, maybe it was Keda.'

The handkerchief caught her eye. There was something strange about it - the engraved letters "GM" and the smell of cologne took her back years. When she picked up the doll, she felt even more puzzled. The face, the dress, the hat and the bow; it was just too much - she just had to say something.

'Where did these come from?' No one answered. 'My uncle had a handkerchief like this, with the same initials and this doll reminds me of my doll Betty that I lost many years ago. It looks as new as the day I lost it!'

'Really!' said Mel, who had been observing her discreetly. 'How long ago was that?'

'A long, long time ago - when I was probably about your age - I lost it shortly after my lovely, Aunt Rubena gave it to me. Grandma Cee paused and smiled, 'She always made me lovely frilly dresses. Anyway, I searched the whole place for the doll but never found it.'

Mel cleared his throat. 'Maybe you should keep them Grandma, and treat them as mysterious gifts from the past.'

'But how did they get here? That's what I want to know!'

Aunty Keda entered the room holding a Julie mango in her slender palm, just as Grandpa Dee found his. 'Where did these come from?' they both asked.

'I don't know,' said Mikal, crossing his fingers behind his back. 'But maybe you should all put your feet up later and enjoy them.'

'Maybe next time this donator will see fit to donate some cash,' Grandpa Dee mumbled. 'I definitely wouldn't say no to that.'

❧Chapter 33: Golden Seasons❧

$\mathcal{T}$he next day after breakfast and chores, the boys rushed to the garden to meet the magic trees. Sometime later, they arrived in a strong easterly breeze that filled the garden.

'Howdy noble partners,' said the feisty Birchard in a Texas drawl; all that was missing was a Texan hat.

'Very funny Birchard, you do know that you are late!'

'Late! Who's late?' he replied. 'We trees are never late Mikal; we're seasonal folks for goodness sake. We do things on time with the seasons.

Before they had time to think about this, the boys instantly found themselves transported to a sun-lit field; full of trees with shiny new leaves. In a flash, the leaves were fully, grown on branches stretching high under the hot sky.

Seconds later, they were a splendid, withering gold beneath their feet, leaving the branches bare, and just as quickly, the branches frosted over from icy winds that left them shivering in their shorts.

'Come on guys, what you playing at!'

'Just getting you into the picture!' said Birchard with a mischievous grin.

'You know what's funny,' he continued as Mel and Mikal miraculously, zoomed back to reality. 'In the dead of winter- our vacation time - that's when we silly trees, decide to strip off and go bald. Burr! Can you believe it! Even the birds abandon us then.'

'They're pretty smart really,' said Mel, rubbing his arms and legs to warm up. They fly off to where it is warm. I could do with that right now.'

'Are you guys ready to go now?' said Elmstead. 'Why are we always dilly-dallying?'

ᔐChapter 34: The Gambian River Boatᔒ

With the boys secured in their branch seats, the trees took to the air like before to enter the bright vortex. When they arrived once again on familiar grounds, Mel and Mikal couldn't wait to find out what new Gambian adventures lay ahead.

From high in the air, there was a spectacular view of the seven hundred mile long, River Gambia, wriggling its way through the land like a long river snake.

Mel's vivid imagination couldn't help picturing it rising up to full height to greet them; hissing menacingly as it exposed huge fangs, before slotting back into place with an enormous, drenching splash. *Huh! That's some greeting!*

Then the trees decided to descend on the riverbed. 'You two will get a good view of the river boats and birds taking off from the river,' said Birchard. He glanced at Mikal, 'And of course, the crocodiles slithering in to go undercover.'

'I am steering clear of them this time,' responded Mikal.

Docked at the edge of the river was an interesting boat-the biggest one in the area - in striking red and blue colours. Mel and Mikal wanted to explore it and since there were no crew on the deck, they seized the opportunity to climb on board.

'All aboard!' Mel said jokingly, when they climbed on deck, having narrowly escaped slipping off the side into the river.

The vacant, well-scrubbed wooden deck had black safety rails on either side. There wasn't much to view there, but the curved staircase leading to the lower deck looked interesting.

'Hello ... is anyone there,' the boys called out before descending the flight of stairs.

The steps creaked as they treaded carefully on each one, but no one seemed alerted to their presence. *Wearing an invisible cape surely pays off!* Mikal thought.

The lower deck had a stack of stuff that they could not identify at a glance and straight ahead was a lower than average door, camouflaged by the wall paint. Mel thought that this might lead to another room or floor below.

Mel turned the knob and the door opened with a rusty

squeak. Inside, the tiny room was dingy and damp - it definitely didn't look like a good place to hang out.

'Let's go back now Mikal. You know how I feel about cold dingy places.'

Mikal responded in his usual manner. 'What's the problem? Let's have a look, it won't take long.' The room lit up when they flicked the light switch, bringing the whole area into view. Barrels, ropes, bottles, crates and large canvas bags were crammed onto the damp floor, leaving very little space to manoeuvre.

Mikal opened one of the bags and white lumpy stuff spilled out. He rubbed a sample between his fingers; it felt moist and sticky. Mel opened another bag with contents that he recognised - rice! He tripped over another bag and slammed into a barrel that toppled over on the floor

They heard footsteps as they decided to leave and a male voice from above said clearly in English, 'Did you hear something below?'

'I didn't hear anything,' another man said. The boys heard him laugh as he said, 'Maybe it's a rat!'

'Hmmm, we don't want rats climbing up on deck now do we!' the first man replied.

Heavy footsteps stomped along the deck and continued down the stairs, feeling alarmed, the boys looked for somewhere to hide, but there was no need. In a few seconds, the door to the storage room slammed shut; the lock clicked and the heavy footsteps ascended the stairs.

'Huh, they've locked us in!' said Mel. 'How are we going to get out? The trees won't be able to find us.' They tugged on the door handle, twisting and turning it repeatedly, but it would not budge.

Banging on the door they shouted, 'Let us out ... we're locked in,' but no one responded, and things felt a lot worse when they heard an engine starting up.

'Oh my days the boat is pulling out. Where is it going?'

'I don't know,' Mikal snapped.

'We've got to find a way out of here,' said Mel, but a little voice in his head told him that was not going to happen just yet. 'We might never get back to the trees or get back home,' he said, thinking about their predicament.

The boat rocked from the river waves lashing against its side as it pulled out, and they slumped to the cabin floor defeated. There was nothing they could do, except sit it out until the door was unlocked, and then what? They didn't have a clue!

Lunch and their rescue were a long way off, so with nothing else to do they nodded off. Sometime after, a sudden jerk in the boat and voices from above awaken them.

'What is this boat doing so far out from the main port,' a man said in a Gambian accent. 'Show us your papers. We can't let you get off the boat if you don't have your papers.'

'What type of cargo are you carrying?' another man asked. The tone of his voice had less authority than the first. 'Do you have papers for this, and are there passengers on board?'

'No, there are no passengers - just cargo, but we have our papers.'

They all stopped talking when they heard banging below.

'Help, open the door, get us out of here,' Mel and Mikal yelled.

'Is that banging and shouting we can hear?'

'I don't know,' one of the boatmen answered. 'Did you let anyone on board?' he asked the other man.

'No, I was with you; I didn't see anyone get on,' he replied. Mel and Mikal banged and shouted again.

'They sound like children,' said the man with more authority in his tone. 'Excuse me, get out of my way. We had better check this out. Have you kidnapped them? Kidnapping is against the law you know.'

'Kidnapped them! What is this … are you accusing us now of kidnapping children?'

Mel and Mikal kept banging on the door with a bottle and shouted even louder when they heard footsteps rushing down the stairs.

The footsteps stopped right by the door. Someone tugged on it and said firmly 'Where are the keys?'

The boys heard keys jangling and then one turning in the lock. They were getting ready to rush through in their invisible state when the door burst opened.

'Hey, what are you boys doing here with those bottles?' said one of the men. 'Are you going to attack someone?'

Mel and Mikal looked down on themselves and realised their capes had fallen off yet again, as they slept - this is why the men could hear them banging.

'Oh boy!' they both cried out.

The two men were dressed in black trousers and black shirts with shoulder badges that had stripes. They looked serious, but did not appear to be carrying any weapons for defence.

'Are you coppers?' Mel asked.

'Coppers, what's that?' one of them asked.

He had three stripes on his shirt, so Mikal figured that he was probably the Chief or a Sergeant. 'He meant, are you policemen,' said Mikal.

'What do you think we look like?' he said sharply. 'Show us your papers. Have you been kidnapped?'

'No Sir. We were locked in by accident.'

The Chief noticed the two open sacks on the floor and went to investigate. 'What's this?' Are you two smugglers? My god, they are getting younger and younger these days.'

'We're not smugglers, we just got locked in,' said Mel.

The Chief ignored Mel's comments and pointed to the sacks. 'Are these your cargo?' he asked the boatmen.

The boys were shocked when the men said, 'No, we've never seen those before.'

'Show me your passports or papers,' the other police officer said to the boys. He only had two stripes on his shirt, so according to Mikal's calculations, he was of lower rank - a Corporal maybe!

'We don't have our passports. We were just looking around and these men accidentally locked us in.'

'Aha! So you two are smugglers and these men have kidnapped you to steal your cargo.'

Mikal felt confused. 'What are you talking about? We don't know anything about what's in here or, smuggling.'

As Mikal argued with them, Mel sneaked away to find their invisible capes. He slipped one on; crept up behind Mikal and draped the other cape over his shoulders and Mikal disappeared right before the Sergeant's eyes.

'Eh! Where did they go? They are magicians as well as smugglers. Find them,' the Chief ordered his colleague, who was not sure what had just taken place. 'I'll handcuff these two; I think they are definitely up to something.'

Mel and Mikal slipped out quietly, climbed over the side of the boat like before, and headed ashore. Would they make it back to their magic trees? They were not sure, but they were certainly going to try.

Chapter 35 Escape to Senegal

They heard the sound of a whistle and the voice of the Chief policeman shouting, 'They've escaped you stupid fool. Find them! Don't let those smugglers or magicians get away; find them!'

Everyone in the area stopped to see what was going on, as Mel and Mikal walked away undetected. They knew that as long as their capes stayed on, it would hide their visibility, however, there was still the problem of getting back to the magic trees.

In despair, Mikal wiped his hands over his face, touching his lips and accidentally, tasted the white stuff stuck to his hand. 'Yuck! What is this? I think it is from the sack. 'It tastes like the flour Grandma uses to make those bland, dumplings without sugar; I don't know how she eats that stuff.'

'Why would those men deny that they were carrying flour and rice cargo?' said Mikal.

'Maybe they stole the boat Mel!'

'Yeah ... maybe they stole the cargo!'

Dusk was rapidly approaching, with no hope of the magic trees, rescuing the boys. On reflection, they had only themselves to blame. They should have told the trees that they were going to explore the boat or, ask permission even. Now getting a lift to Banjul from this remote area was very unlikely - they were going to have to spend a night under the stars.

Feeling tired and hungry, they decided to rest beneath some covers on the back of an abandoned truck. They helped themselves to sandwiches, drinks and apples that luckily someone had stashed under the covers and soon nodded off.

Sometime later, they awoke to see the truck travelling in the still of the night through the countryside, with hardly anyone in sight. It chugged along the road like the car in the film *"Chitty Chitty Bang Bang"*, any minute now it could fall apart!

'That's great!' Mikal sighed. 'Now we're truly lost!'

They were contemplating whether to jump off the truck and find some other way to get back to Banjul, when they saw bright city lights on the horizon.

'Thank goodness, we'll soon find some kind of life around here,' said Mikal.

The driver parked up in the city; muttering something about a punctured tyre and strolled off without realising he had passengers. Now Mel and Mikal were alone in the big city, with no idea of what to do next.

The streetlight on the corner flashed on and off on a signpost that said "Welcome to Dakar".

'We must be in Senegal,' said Mikal.

'Great! Now we are even further away from the trees. We'll never get home and I am very hungry,' said Mel.

Mikal suddenly remembered that Grandpa Dee's sister; their Great Aunt Viviane lived in Senegal but he wasn't sure where. They were going to have to find her sooner than later, but for now, they would stay hidden in the truck until morning.

Interestingly, this modern looking city was buzzing from the break of dawn when Mel and Mikal decided to search for food. As the sun rose higher in the sky, there was so much more to look at, lots of tall buildings, busy roads with cars and taxis tooting for people to get out of the way.

Traders speaking Wolof, French and other languages, were busy setting up their market stalls. This gave the invisible boys the chance to eat whatever they fancied, each time promising themselves to get some CFA Francs later to pay for the cost.

It was around 10:30am that as luck would have it; Mel and Mikal heard a female voice in the crowd that they both recognised. They followed the sound of the voice; through the stalls, until suddenly there she was, bargaining with a trader. *What a relief!*

Aunt Viviane was a very classy, beautiful and attractive, dark skinned woman. She was quite tall and always well dressed, regardless of the occasion. Dressed in a bright, red African outfit, with matching headdress cleverly tied around her forehead; she clearly stood out from the crowd.

She had met them many times back home, so all they needed to do was to find something or somewhere to hide their capes before they approached her. The plastic bag they had just spotted was just the thing!

They tapped her gently on the back unsure of how she would respond. She spun around immediately and looked at them over her glasses.

'Hey ... what do you want?' she said. 'Are you looking for something?' She peered at them more closely. 'Wait a minute, how strange; you boys look so much like my nephews.'

'It's us Aunt Viviane,' said Mikal.

'Oh my goodness - it so nice to see you!' she said, embracing them. 'Did you come with your Grandpa or your mum and dad?'

'We came alone Auntie,' said Mikal. 'We got stranded on a boat from the River Gambia and ended up here. We need to get back there quickly so that we can get home.'

'What! What are you talking about? You could not have arrived here without one of them. Did you get lost? '

'We came without them and then got lost,' said Mel

'You came here by yourselves ... but how?'

'It's a long story Aunty, if we told you, you wouldn't believe us, but we need help.'

'Well, try me! I want to know what's going on right now,' she said firmly. She paid for her shopping and led them to her car. The boys seated themselves quietly in the back, not uttering a word or attempting to challenge her.

Minutes later, she pulled up in front of a large house and

parked the car in the drive facing a nicely painted veranda. She invited the boys into her well-decorated living room, coordinated with modern sofas, solid oak furniture, and beautifully framed pictures portraying African culture.

Aunt Viviane offered them homemade lemonade, whilst lunch was being prepared, and the boys smiled as this brought back memories of the escapade in their Uncle Sanji's kitchen.

Mikal picked up a magazine from the coffee table. 'Look at this, I didn't know that Senegal surrounds The Gambia and, it says here the Wolof group is the largest in the country- forty three percent of the population!'

'Wish we could stay a bit longer to explore the place, but maybe we'll have an adventure here next summer.'

'We're having one right now,' Mikal replied.

Aunt Viviane and her housekeeper were great cooks. They offered them a choice of rice, served with Chep-bu-jen; the delicious national dish, which was actually fish, cooked in tomato sauce, with vegetables and green peppers, or, Yassa - grilled chicken, with lemon juice, pepper and onions, and they sample both of these delicious dishes.

After they had eaten, she pulled up a chair; perched her

glasses onto her nose, and this time she wasn't messing around; she wanted answers right now.

'Well you see Aunty, Mel wished that the Birch and Elm trees in our Grandparents neighbour's garden could talk, and they came alive, with magical powers that can take us flying in the air and through a vortex. They can even time travel...'

'Wow! Hold on ... I want the truth, not fairy tales,' she said, flashing her eyes. Somehow, when she did that, a picture of their Aunty Keda came to mind.

'But I am telling the truth Aunty - I knew you wouldn't believe us.'

'Ok, so where are these trees now Mikal? If they have magical powers, why haven't they found you since you left yesterday?'

'We left them on the banks of the river when we climbed on the boat. They normally rescue us but we're not sure why they haven't this time.'

'This is why we had to find you,' confirmed Mel.

'And I'm glad you did, but I'm going to call my brother Dee - your Grandpa. He should know what is going on with you two. You've travelled all this way without a chaperone and could have been hurt or even kidnapped with no one to protect you.'

'Uh Oh! Please don't do that Aunty. Grandpa doesn't know about our magic trees; he doesn't even know that we're here,' said Mikal.

'Well it's about time that he did!' She got up to use the telephone in the living room and uttered a very controlled and lady-like shriek as she entered, followed by 'Oh my goodness!'

The boys rushed into the living room along with the housekeeper and were all shocked to see Birchard and Elmstead with their heads almost touching the ceiling, sitting on the sofa with a cup of tea in their hands. The housekeeper instantly fainted.

'Good day to you Madam,' they both said.

'Sorry about your housekeeper,' said Elmstead. 'She'll come around soon. Hope you don't mind us sipping a cup of your lovely green tea. We are developing quite a taste for this stuff. With a bit of sugar, it tastes almost like our glucose. I must say though, your china cups are quite exquisite.'

'Who are you?' she said, stepping awkwardly over her

Housekeeper. 'What are you weird looking creatures doing in my living room? Did you two break in? Maybe I am missing something here. Is there some sort of celebration taking place and you are dressed as masquerades to perform there?'

The trees continued to sip their tea without responding; after all, they were "Guardians" not thieves - and the thought of being mistaken for masquerades was very humiliating.

'Wait a minute ... why am I asking you creatures such questions,' said Aunt Vivienne. 'This isn't real - maybe I'm dreaming or maybe - you're just in my imagination, like the song says.'

'Should we pinch her to confirm that she's awake?' said Birchard.

'No ... I think you had better not,' Elmstead said solemnly.

Mel and Mikal could not contain themselves any longer. They rushed over to the trees to get an answer to their question. 'Where have you been? We were stuck in a boat and couldn't get back, but you didn't come to get us.'

'Well first of all, let us ask the questions,' Birchard

replied calmly, in a tone that resonated all around them. 'Where have you been? You disappeared without telling us. We had to track you down.

'Maybe we have to put a microchip with a signal in your hand so we can find you;' said Elmstead. 'But I am sure you wouldn't appreciate having that gross, micro accessory invading your being!'

'What's going on here? Do you know these horrible creatures?'

'They are not horrible Aunty; they're our magic trees and we love them,' said Mel.

'What! You love them! Eh boy! Are you crazy? I'm going to call the police to get them out of here right now and then your Grandpa Dee.'

Elmstead placed his cup on the table and said, 'Madam, they have told you the truth. We are their travel guardians with magical powers and, we protect them, regardless of how it seems. If not, we wouldn't have found them today.'

'That's correct!' said Birchard. 'Were do you think we were when you were locked in the boat cabin? On the deck! And we knew everything you did down there. We left you food under the covers of that old truck last night; flew above it and stood guard as you slept to ensure that you came to no harm.

'The only time you were left alone,' added Elmstead, 'was when you slipped through time from the mango tree and when you ventured into the cave. Also, when you were stranded on the deserted beach, after we were stuck in the Earth's core. However, you seemed to have coped pretty well without us each time!'

'My nephews were in a cave with Ratbats, slipped through time, and you all got stuck in the earth's core, whilst they were stranded on a deserted beach; are you two as crazy as you look? Someone needs to explain, and it had better be the police.' She picked up the telephone and started dialling.

'Oh Elmstead, why did you have to say that? Now look what you have done! Madam, could you please put the phone down and listen for a minute.'

'No ... I've done all the listening I'm going to do today. My Housekeeper is out cold and I am going to call the police to get you two out of my house. After you leave, my husband and I will see to it that our nephews are returned safely home.'

Birchard placed his tea on the coffee table. 'Ok Madam, we've tried, but you've left us with no choice.' He clicked his fingers three times and Aunty Viviane immediately stopped what she was about to do, and looked as if she had gone into a trance right where she stood. He clicked his fingers again and the unconscious Housekeeper drifted from the floor unto the sofa.

'Sit your Aunt on the sofa next to her housekeeper,' said Birchard. 'I'm going to let them both fall into a deep sleep and when they wake up; they won't remember a thing.

Aunt Viviane lay sleeping on the sofa along with the housekeeper, looking as peaceful as a lamb. The boys covered her with a shawl, kissed her on the cheek and whispered, 'Bye Aunty thank you for the lunch. We will see you when you next come to visit Grandpa Dee.'

Mel and Mikal closed the front door and flew off with their magic trees. Soaring through the skies once again was a great feeling and they were relieved, to be back in the branches of their magic trees.

❧Chapter 36: The Market Vase❧

*A*rriving back in The Gambia, the magic trees flew over some of the famous markets as well as the village of Juffure - Kunta Kinte's village, and the boys were spared some of the sordid details of their historical roots.

The Royal Albert Market in Banjul was famous just like the Serekunda Market. It had greatly expanded since its beginnings, with a few female traders on the street.

'Did Prince Albert start the Royal Albert Market too?'

'I'm not sure Mel, but maybe he came to the 1965 Independence celebration.'

'Really... I wish I could see that.' Something "pinged" as Mel said this. 'What was that?' he asked.

'Just a chime,' Birchard chuckled.

The Royal Albert Market stalls sold many fascinating things that the boys wanted to see, so the tress agreed to let them look around and meet up with them in 30 minutes. The rug designs, beautiful printed fabrics, ornaments and spices on display were just some of the things they admired.

It was quite amusing observing the locals skilfully bargaining with traders to get their preferred price.

'How much is this dish?' an elegant woman in a bright blue African dress and Tiko head wrap enquired.

'15 Dalasi,' the trader replied

'I only have 10,' replied the woman. 'Will you take it, or should I try elsewhere?' The trader stood shaking his head, as he watched her walked off happily with the goods.

The boys strolled invisibly in and out of the amazing market stalls, sidestepping tourists and native Gambians, but bumping into a few, who were puzzled, by the unseen, mysterious, obstacles in their path.

Mel checked his watch. 'We'd better get back now. '30 minutes is almost up.'

Minutes later, they were still trying to make their way out of the market - they had been going around in circles. In despair, they stopped at a stall with ornamental vases, to retrace their steps, and that's when the incident happened.

Mel accidentally tripped and knocked an expensive

ornamental vase off its perch. It fell with an almighty crash, scattering fragments everywhere. For a moment, there was instant silence. Onlookers stopped what they were doing and gathered around the stall. Some began the task of cleaning it up, but the boys, surrounded from all angles, could not escape.

They were pushing against a forceful obstacle blocking their path and could not move an inch forward. Trying to go around it did not help; it moved in the same direction. Looking up, a tall man of huge proportion stood before them. He bounced the mysterious, invisible objects in his path with his large abdomen that was as solid as a packed barrel.

Pushing his spectacles further up on his nose, he kept clutching at the space in front of him as the boys swayed out of his reach. He wore an expensive pair of trendy sunglasses that the boys thought might have futuristic lens. This could probably explain why he could see faint images of them, even though they were invisible.

When his hands landed on top of their heads, he shouted, 'Ah ha ... I've got you now!' The boys winced as he gripped their hairs tightly, pulling painfully on the roots.

'We should have gone to the barbers,' Mel yelled.

They stamped on his foot as hard as they could and attempted to escape, but somehow he managed to grab them before they got away. Pulling himself up with the boys in tow, he lifted them off their feet, similar to Carlos, the Jamaican hotel ghost, who at least could disappear.

'I have the rogues here - the culprits! Call security or the police,' he shouted to the crowd. 'They are firmly in my grasp; they can't get away.'

No one moved. The onlookers wondered what he was ranting on about, with arms and clenched fist, positioned some distance from either side of his stomach. He seemed to be holding on to something not visible to the naked eye.

'Perhaps he's seeking attention,' some onlookers remarked.

From where they stood, there were no culprits, just a larger than average, wealthy man, with an oversized abdomen. Another kick to the man's shin loosened his grip. The boys dived to the ground and almost got away again, but he reached out and grabbed the back of their necks. *He must have X-ray vision,* Mikal thought. Then things changed.

A voice with a recognisable, tone bellowed 'RELEASE

THEM!'

The man looked up in the air and all around, with the boys still clinched in his grip, frantically trying to identify the source of the sound that only he and the boys could hear. Seconds later, Birchard repeated his command in slow motion and his amplified Dart Vader - Optimus Prime tone had a much greater effect.

His tone boomed through the air like dynamite, creating sound waves that rattled the stalls and shook the ground.

'Earthquake,' yelled some of the traders, who felt the effects of the tone, but could not hear the sound.

The man's grasp on the boys suddenly weakened and they tumbled to the floor. He twisted and turned looking right then left, but nothing he could see was capable of making the sound that injected such fear into his being.

The whole, fearful incident proved to be too much; he gasped, clutched the front of his trousers and seized the chance to escape. The boys felt sorry for him at this point, even though their arms, necks and scalps ached dreadfully.

As he went passed the female traders they whispered, 'Poor thing, maybe he's just having a bad day!

❦Chapter 37: The Carved Mask❧

Leaving the events of the famous Albert Market behind, the trees and the boys continued their journey in the summer heat.

A few miles from Banjul, popular beaches like Cape Point, and fancy hotels in the town of Bakau, known for its botanical gardens, went sailing past.

'Birchard do you think we could spend a night in one of these posh hotels?'

'Is this another wish Mel? If it is, we will have to think about it - because you two might create havoc on the hotel grounds, just like the Albert Market.'

'Oh no we won't, we promise that we'll be as good as gold.'

'As good as gold eh,' said Elmstead. 'I wonder how much "Carat" your deeds will weigh up to so far.'

Flying though Brikama, a town famous for its craft market, the boys missed the chance to view the beautiful wooden carvings, because of the previous incident. They were not sure how, but Birchard managed to obtain a rich, mahogany carved mask and placed it in his branches.

Mikal joined Mel in Birchard's branches to view the carving. It was skilfully, carved with black, stemmed headdress; and mouth fixed in a permanent grin. It looked strange, but taking into account the craftsmanship, it was indeed very beautiful.

Mikal blew on the carving and removed the dust with a tissue. When he cleaned the nose, he heard a squeaky sound, which he blamed on the slippery varnish. He passed it to Mel, who felt it jumped.

'Huh! Check this out Mikal ... I think it is alive!'

'What? Don't be silly it's only a piece of wood.'

Mikal picked it up and this time it both squeaked and jumped. He dropped it instantly. 'Aaarrgh! What on earth was that?'

'See ... I told you this thing was alive, Mikal.'

'It can't be! Maybe it is just vibrating like Elmstead said.'

'But we heard it squeaked,' replied Mel.

'Well actually, you wouldn't have felt me jump or heard me squeak if this here tree didn't magic me up from his trunk. And, if you young man, didn't blow your breath right into my nostrils to contaminate me.'

Mikal was so shocked. 'Who said that?'

'Well who do you think? Look at me!'

'You can talk!'

'Yes, but only because I was carved from your magic tree and you blew on me; so am part of Birchard and part of you.'

'Whoa ... hold on! You're part of me?' 'Yes ... I have your voice - weren't you listening? Now I look like a piece of African craft, but speak with an English Accent like you. What a sorrowful state I'm in.'

'Ahem! Does that mean you have magical powers like Birchard?' asked Mel.

'Yes,' the mask replied wearily. 'I'm going to end up sounding like a right idiot if you all keep making me say "Yes" all the time. What is your wish?'

'Wish ... who said anything about a wish ... we're just trying to figure you out. Anyway, how would we know, if you are a baddie or a goodie?'

'I don't even know myself. Let's hope I have not inherited Birchard's or this young man's negative qualities.'

'Hahaha, you mean like Birchard's temper and Mikal's habit of always breaking the rules.'

'Yeah right! I tell you what,' said Mikal. 'You can't go squeaking and jumping when you're touched - you'll frighten people - you're only a piece of carving! If you wish, we could make you a leaf bag and you can stay in the tree and hang around with us.'

The Mask jumped at the thought, 'I would like that!' it replied.

'What would you like us to call you?' asked Mel

'How about Craftee or Maskee,' the mask suggested. 'Pronounced as Mas...kee?'

'Let's settle for Mas...kee,' said Mikal. 'We don't want to hang out with any "Craftee" beings.'

'Ok that's settled then, you are the boss,' Maskee replied.

❧Chapter 38: The Mighty Centurion❧

*A*rriving in Banjul once more, their quest was to find Grandpa Dee's parents; and Mikal was the first to spot the street sign pointing to Hagan Street, where they had lived.

'Great! Now all we have to do is find their old house,' said Mikal.

'We can do that! We could also take it a step further and go back in time to when they lived here,' said Birchard.

'That would be awesome, but try not to get into any glitches, hurricanes, or create earthquakes this time.'

Mikal gulped when Birchard sternly replied, 'We will try, if you ease up on the disappearing acts and rescue calls?'

With all agreed the trees switched on their time travel compass and prepared for routine take off. When they landed, surprisingly they were on a moonlight road.

'Why are we in the dark? Is this another navigational

glitch? You can't blame us this time.'

'Just chill Mel. We are still in Banjul but in 1965. It's the 18th February- Independence Day. Sorry ... I meant Independence Night!'

'Oh my gosh Birchard, you granted it!'

'You look surprised. Didn't you get confirmation from the Wish Chime? I heard it!'

'The Wish Chime! You mean that "ping" sound. So that's what it was.'

'We may also consider your request to spend the night in a hotel, but that depends...'

'On what Elmstead?'

'Your behaviour, you have to gain your rewards!'

Mel and Mikal shook their heads and walked off with a heavy sigh.

'I see Maskee is relaxing comfortably in his leaf bag, so I guess, you'll have some company whilst we travel.'

'Birchard … have you been eavesdropping again? This must be what they call Guardian Control,' replied Mel.

The Gambian Independence ceremony was due to take place in under an hour, in the village of Brikama -the place with the famous craft market.

'We have to get there on time, unless you want to turn up embarrassingly as a latecomer. We will leave as soon as we switch on our navigating compass lights.'

'Navigating compass lights! We didn't know you had that Elmstead.'

'I guess not Mel. We have never travelled at night before; you're usually tucked up in bed. Come on, let's get moving!'

The trees switched on the compass lights in their trunks and they shun bright like an inner sun; sending streams of light ahead of them to light the path of their root steps.

'Is there no end to your magical powers?' Mikal asked.

'We have limits as magic trees, but as mentioned before

we're constantly evolving with great powers of thought.'

Something flashed in Mikal's mind just then (a solution to a previous puzzle) but he decided to mention it to Elmstead later, when it was more appropriate.

They set out on their journey to the ceremony in the still of the night, quickly covering the distance with the help of the magic trees' huge strides.

'Why didn't they fly?' whispered Mel. 'Maybe they prefer to stay grounded to avoid bumping into things in the air.'

'Or maybe it's because there are fewer people around to step on their root-laced boots. Hahaha! Shush, they might hear us Mel.'

A yellow bush taxi drove by, bumping up and down the quiet country road, with passengers chatting loudly inside. Minutes later, they leapt out of the way of a chauffeur driven limousine, speeding past with blazing headlights, probably carrying a very distinguished guest.

As the trees hurried along, the strange sounds of insects combined with their clumping root-steps, reminded the boys of the Jamaican night tales. Monkeys startled by their presence leapt through the trees lining the road, and the creepy shadows of their branches, swaying to a light breeze, made them huddle in their branch seats.

The road suddenly curved and a huge, strange looking tree stood in the middle blocking their path. The moonlight cast a shadow on its silhouette and the boys noted that its trunk was much wider than both of the magic trees' combined.

At first, the boys thought it had grown there and they would have to fly above it, but they became concerned when they saw Birchard and Elmstead whispering just before their inner compass lights unexpectedly faded. Then, the trees pulled out wooden, batons from somewhere in their trunks that the boys had failed to notice before.

Quite unexpectedly, they heard a strange sound coming from the huge tree, as if it was straining to lift weights in a gym; then a weird, face popped up in its upper trunk. Its face had stern, grey eyes similar to its trunk that stared at the magic trees without blinking.

Moments later, its stiff lips parted with a struggle, and it surprisingly spoke in a deep voice that had much less resonance than Birchard's. 'Greetings travellers, I am the Centurion; sent here as a guard from a realm known as The Plane of Force.'

'Greetings Centurion, my name is Birchard and this is my friend Elmstead. We are on our way to an important ceremony and will need to pass through.'

'Anything magical passing by me at this time, depending on their character, have to either pay me a toll or engage in a brawl. You two, will only, be given the option of a brawl. What say you?'

'We had a feeling we'd be faced with a challenge, and suspected we'd get the worst deal. So, as we have no other option but to continue our journey, we'll engage in a brawl, as long as there is fair play,' said Birchard.

'Tell me what are you put here to guard?' said Elmstead.

'I've kept this country road safe for centuries; preventing all sorts of weird things from navigating through here and scaring ordinary folks. Now you two look like the scary, mischievous type.'

'Oh really … look who is talking!' said Elmstead. 'Now, I am going to ask you this once; would you let us pass without a fight?'

'No … rules are rules; even though they can be broken,' replied the Centurion with a slight, menacing giggle.

'What are the rules,' asked Elmstead.

'Quite simply, if you rise to the challenge and get injured to the point where you can't continue the fight, you will lose and therefore won't be able to pass through here now, or, at any other time during the night, on foot or in the air.'

'If I get injured and can't continue the fight, which is unlikely since I'm twice the size of you both; you have my word as the Centurion and guardian of this road that I will let you pass unharmed.'

'I see!' said Elmstead. 'I think you boys had better whip out Maskee from his leaf bag, and ask him to move you to a secure spot. I had a distinct feeling this path would be dangerous.'

True to their request, Maskee whisked the boys into a safe spot. Actually, he placed them in a swaying hammock that they were either hanging out of, or struggling to sit up straight in it, to watch what was about to take place.

The Centurion pulled out four, huge branch arms two on either side of his trunk, with similar batons to the magic trees.

'Let the battle commence,' he said, looking very pleased with himself.

'I don't believe it! Mikal, we are going to see magic trees

battling right here in the woods.'

The battle started at a whizzing speed and the boys could hardly see what was happening, until Maskee granted their wish for more light. It then became amazing to watch; almost like a comedy sketch.

They all seemed equally matched, each giving as good as they get. The Centurion as chunky as he appeared, was very quick, strong and as light on his feet as a ballerina. In fact, the leaves surrounding his mid-trunk could easily pass for a ballerina's Tutu. He jumped through the air doing spins as if he was dancing to Swan Lake and tried to land blows on the magic trees with every spin.

Birchard and Elmstead were surprisingly just as quick; blocking blows from his four batons as they flew up in the air, twisting and turning like famous Kung Fu experts. Then things changed and the stakes were raised.

Birchard and Elmstead had to step aside when a ray of blue light unexpectedly came from nowhere. It surrounded the Centurion hovering in the air, until he glowed with sparks flying in all directions.

After the light disappeared, he flexed his branches like a boxer, getting ready for a fight. He appeared stronger, which left the magic trees wishing they had back-up support. Where was their Godlink when they needed him?

He swung his batons forcefully; almost knocking out Birchard and Elmstead, several times, which left the boys fearing for their safety. One solid blow and they would be the losers. Their quick levitation speed, allowed them more than once, to avoid these knockout blows.

They wrestled in mid-air and lashed out at the Centurion until he placed them in a headlock. This wasn't looking good! To be defeated now would simply be disastrous for the magic trees; they had to come up with a plan quickly.

The Centurion was on the verge of victory when quite suddenly a dreadful sound exploded in the air. The earth shook from the tremor and the boys tumbled out of their hammock along with Maskee. It was amazing!

They couldn't figure out, if it was Birchard's Dart Vader -Optimus Prime tone, amplified a hundred times over that took the centurion by surprise, or if a supreme, force assisted them. Then they had a lingering thought, *it must have been The Seer - their Godlink!*

The amplified sound expelled an energy that was so strong; it forced the Centurion's arms apart from around their necks and left him stunned.

Spotting their chance to claim victory, the magic trees seized the Centurion in his moment of weakness; knowing that if they allowed him to regain his powers, they would be done for! So, with every ounce of strength they dived to the ground and pinned him down.

'Game over pal,' Birchard said in his ear.

Elmstead moved his head closer to the Centurion's face as he struggled to free himself.

'Listen oh mighty one, as a great English man once sung, "The harder they come, the harder they fall" so although...'

'Actually, to be precise Elmstead it was the great Jamaican singer, Jimmy Cliff, get it right - give him credit!'

'Quite right ... my apologies!' said Elmstead. 'As I was saying, although it wasn't easy and we're injured from your lethal blows, we won the battle fair and square by your rules so, let's just end this now and we'll be on our way.

'Elmstead and I hate fights and will only engage in it to defend ourselves. We are too injured to continue this battle and with all due respect Centurion, neither can you. So, please let us through, we have an important ceremony to attend.'

The dazed Centurion tried to pull himself up, but the magic trees held him down firmly. 'Disappointedly you are both the winners,' he said. 'But, I will honour my promise as I normally do.' He touched his hands against theirs and said, 'I was wrong about you, but we're all kindred folks, and since you've now gained my respect, you're free to go!'

Birchard and Elmstead responded in the same manner, 'Respect to you too mighty Centurion and may you protect this area for many years to come.'

The Centurion sighed heavily then grinned a bit mischievously and disappeared without a trace, right from beneath the magic trees, who fell flat on their faces.

'Well fancy that Birchard! He could have escaped all this time we thought we had him pinned downed. Who would have guessed that he is the decent, honourable type? Maybe he comes from good, supreme stock.'

'That's why it's said you should never judge a tree by its bark or, a book by its cover. I wonder who said that originally!'

'Who cares Birchard? Let's go we have a grand ceremony to attend.'

*D*espite the Centurion hold up they arrived at the ceremony on time, to join the well-dressed crowd making their way to the grand ceremonial building.

The atmosphere was charged with excitement! Mainly because the ceremony was due to be celebrated with distinguished guests - The Prime Minister Dawda K. Jawara, Governor Sir John Paul and the Duke and Duchess of Kent; representing the Queen of England.

To Gambians, this was indeed a grand, state affair called *"The Mans Bengo"* meaning *"The Gathering of Kings"*. Mel was disappointed to find out that Prince Albert, who had a Gambian market named after him, was nowhere in sight.

However, they entered the building and seated themselves, whilst Birchard, Elmstead and Maskee observed the ceremony from outside.

'This is awesome!' said Mikal. 'We have to be on our best behaviour.'

Mel laughed. 'Yeah, we have to measure up to those "Carats" Elmstead spoke about.'

The boys listened as musicians dressed in matching traditional outfits, skilfully played their drums to herald the arrival of the VIPs.

Grand chairs made from the finest materials, seated the important guests and the Prime Minster and Governor carefully removed their shoes as a mark of respect before greeting them.

When the prolonged speeches finally ended, the lowering of the Union Jack and its replacement with the Gambian flag, to the song of the Gambian National Anthem, led to cheers from the crowd.

Somewhere amongst the crowd, their Great Grandparents Yande and Ensa rose from their seats, and proudly made their way to the entrance; feeling very elated; but totally unaware of the two, related time travellers in their midst.

Feeling in awe of what had just taken place; the boys with their faces beaming in the moonlight, shared their gratitude and excitement with the trees

'It was really great! I don't think we'll ever forget this.'

'We certainly hope not,' said Elmstead. 'Come to think of it, this experience was really an extremely magical one. You've just witnessed and showed respect for a great occasion in Gambian History that some people didn't live to see.'

'Someday when you're called Grandpa Miky and Mele, it will be your turn to tell your grandchildren all about this,' Birchard chuckled.

Mel and Mikal stared at him, and from the look on their faces, it was evident that they were not amused. 'Maybe we won't have to tell them,' replied Mel. 'We'll just tune into their thoughts.'

On that note, Mikal felt that it was now the right time, to reveal his solution to the puzzle he had mentioned earlier. 'You know it took me a while, but I've finally figured out, how you both made me have that dream encounter, with the Arawaks or Tainos in Jamaica.'

'Really!' said Elmstead.

'Yeah, and if you remember, I promised to let you know when I did.'

'Quite right,' replied the trees.

'It's the same method you used to tune into our thoughts, or, let us hear your voices in our heads. Come on now... we're not stupid; we both know that you do that.'

'I see!' both trees replied.

'I figured that when I was under the coconut tree in Jamaica, Birchard put me into a drowsy state through hypnosis that's why I saw the hazy scene first.

Then, Elmstead took an entire scene of the Tainos' or Arawaks history and injected it telepathically into my mind. Only, I thought I was dreaming; but I was actually experiencing part of an era stored in his history banks. Now that was very clever guys!'

'Well, we'd say the same for you,' said Elmstead. 'You need to be very clever to figure that out - we're impressed! Now, just think of how easy it would be to deal with Maths or scientific lessons, if you use those powers of deduction in class.'

❧Chapter 40: The Overnight Hotel❧

They boys and the magic trees, left the ceremonial building feeling very merry after they sampled, some of the delicious, midnight snacks and drinks.

'We have two more wishes to grant you before returning home,' said Birchard. 'First, because of your good behaviour, we'll grant your "overnight hotel stay" request, and search for your Great Grandparents tomorrow.'

'We have a surprise for you both that you'll find out about later,' continued Elmstead, 'Which will be the last of the adventures for this summer.'

The trees navigated their way with their inner compass, with the boys in their branches, until they came upon a traditional style, grand hotel in the midst of a park, surrounded by beautiful trees and shrubs. Lights streamed through the many windows on the top and bottom floors, whilst guests, seated around fully, laid tables with various dishes, filled the dining room.

Peeking through the windows, they spotted a vacant room with long drapes and an inviting bed. Knowing that it was impossible to book a room as guests; they climbed through the window to settle in for the night; whilst the trees and Maskee played their "guardian watching" role, from outside.

It was nearly 2am, so with only a few hours to rest before the next adventure. They washed, got undressed, placed their clothes on the chair and within minutes were fast asleep.

A knock on the door around 7:30am awaken them and a female voice said, 'Room service!' Mel and Mikal huddled quietly under the covers, hoping that the person would go away, but they had no such luck. The person knocked again and repeated a bit louder, 'Room service!'

Mel and Mikal scurried under the bed dressed only in their underwear. A few seconds later, they heard keys rattling and the door opened. A woman dressed in the hotels, housekeeping uniform entered the room.

'Eh! Thought this room was supposed to be empty,' she muttered. 'It looks like the other Housekeeper didn't do her job properly, so now I have another room to clean.'

She set about vacuuming the floor, clearly annoyed about her additional task, whilst Mel and Mikal remained as quiet as a mouse under the bed. Then, Mel blew their cover. He couldn't help sneezing from the dust.

The Housekeeper switched off the vacuum cleaner. 'Who is under there?' Having no response she repeated, 'who is under there and what are you doing down there?'

The boys felt too petrified to move and Mikal felt even worse, when he suddenly realised that they were visible, otherwise Mel's sneeze would have gone unheard.

'The capes Mel … the capes! We left them on the chair before we went to bed; we are visible!' Being so tired, they had placed their invisible capes with their pile of clothes on the chair the night before, without thinking.

The Housekeeper by now was getting quite irritable, 'What did you say? Of course you're visible, and I will see you when you get out from under there.'

Mel and Mikal poked their heads out from under the bed. 'Eh! There are two of you - two young tramps,' she said with contempt. 'Don't you have homes to go to? Where are your parents? On second thoughts, I won't worry about them. I will just call the manager and security to throw you both out.'

She ran out of the room shouting 'Mr Kumareh, come quickly, we have intruders - call security.'

'Oh no, I think we'd better get out Mel. If we get arrested, our Grandparents would have a fit! And we would have a sore behind.'

They felt for their invisible capes amongst the pile of clothes and put them on. Then with T-shirts, trousers and trainers in hand, made a run for the window and jumped onto their magic trees waiting outside.

'Hurry ...you've got to take off,' said the boys to Maskee and the trees. 'The Housekeeper went to get security!'

Unbelievably, the trees actually took off hilariously like an airplane; limping as fast as they could in their root-laced boots through the hotel grounds, before gathering enough speed to take off. It was a very bumpy ride indeed!

The Housekeeper returned just as they cleared the window, and was quite startled to see their clothes and trainers floating higher and higher through the air, as Birchard and Elmstead flew off above the hotel grounds.

'Oh my god, those boys were real ghosts!

The Senior Housekeeper came running into the room.

'Where are they?' she asked.

'They two ghosts disappeared through the window,' said the first Housekeeper, 'I have seen them and heard them talking under the bed before I came to get you ...'

She stopped in mid-sentence as the Senior Housekeeper walked confidently over to the window. She thought the Housekeeper was hysterical, but witnessing the same scene left her stunned. The bodiless, drifting T-shirts and trainers in their flight through the lengthy, hotel grounds seemed to be dancing to an unheard tune.

The Hotel Manager came rushing in behind her and could not believe what he saw either, nor find the words to describe it. This was too much to comprehend and they both collapsed on the floor. What a palaver!

The first Housekeeper looked at the collapsed heap on the floor. 'Eh!' she said mockingly. 'You thought I was just imagining things and now you've seen it, guess what, you've fainted.' She hissed her teeth, stepped proudly over them and walk through the door triumphantly, before locking them in. 'When you both wake up and manage to get out,' she said amusingly, 'I will just blame it on the ghosts!'

$\mathcal{T}$hey cleared the hotel grounds and stopped to rest on the road. 'Told you that you would both create havoc in the hotel,' said Birchard.

'Oh give them a break guys,' said Maskee 'It was the Housekeeper!'

'That's true Birchard. She saw us and went kinda crazy and, we didn't even get to have breakfast.'

'Are you kidding Mikal? Your Breakfast will be fruits from the trees on the roadside.'

After their fruity breakfast, they time travelled back to Hagan Street in 1962 and it looked set for an interesting spring celebration.

Gambians love to celebrate period! Births, weddings and events like the annual Independence Day, the Kartong Music festival, the Homecoming Roots Festival in honour of Bob Marley's birthday and more.

Mel was hoping that they could go to the spring celebrations after they searched for their Great Grandparents and they didn't have to wait long before they spotted their Great Grandma walking out of a house on Hagan Street.

'I have to get to school,' she said to someone inside. 'I don't want to be late for my class.'

She rode off on her bike at a steady speed, with her pink Tiko headdress and matching waist wrap that was almost sweeping the wheel. Many people greeted her on the way.

'Nanga Def Teacher Yande,' meaning, "How are you?"

'Mang Fi Rek,' she replied, meaning, "I am just fine."

Arriving at the school, they were surprised to find that it was the same schoolhouse, Mel had explored on their last visit. It looked grand with its newly fitted windows, fresh coat of paint, and grounds filled with children's laughter.

At 8:30am, the bell rang piercingly, summoning the children in their blue cotton dresses or khaki pants and shirt to class. They found Great Grandma Yande teaching a Maths class that the children seemed to be enjoying. Young Grandpa Dee was at the front of the class answering questions as usual with his brother - their Great Uncle Papis. Mel remembered this classroom well. He had met the caretaker who chased him there. *How uncanny!*

Outside, the sun grew hotter as it rose steadily above their heads. A tree on the school grounds that was not there on Mel's last visit, had insects flying in and out of a hollow part of its trunk, so off he went to investigate.

He was about to climb the tree, when he heard someone approaching. Mel gasped and quickly hid behind a bush. It's was young Grandpa Dee - he had sneaked out of class! He had heard the buzzing sound and had stopped to look. Mel then realised that he was going to beat him to it!

Grandpa Dee sprung up on one of the branches and swung on it like an athlete before climbing up the trunk. He broke of a leafless twig and twirled it around in the hole. Suddenly he jumped back and moved quickly to the other side of the tree trunk, as a swarm of bees charged furiously out of the hole, filling the air with an aggravated buzz.

They hovered around as if looking for the culprit, then

flew towards the schoolhouse, and to Mel's dismay, through the school windows. The children working quietly in their classrooms felt startled by the invasion. They frantically tried to fight off the bees and having no luck, fled to the playground with their teachers behind them.

The bees followed in hot pursuit, filling the air like a grey cloud and causing chaos in the playground. They were all puzzled, but no one had the answer except Mel and of course, young Grandpa Dee. After a long, crazy period, the bees finally returned to their hive in the hollow of the tree.

However, the children were too upset to resume their studies; and realising they were fighting a losing battle; the teachers sent them home to recover. Great Grandma Yande rode off very upset, leaving Grandpa Dee and Uncle Papis to follow on foot. Mikal rescued her gold brooch that had fallen off her top and pocketed it for later.

'I was right. Grandpa did get up to tricks and so did Grandma, stealing the firecracker. 'He got away with it, but she didn't.' Mel suddenly looked amused. 'Maybe I'll get him to confess after all those years. That should be fun!'

❧Chapter 42: The Champion❧

On their way back to the town they passed a tennis court with two players competing in a match that reminded them of the Wimbledon Championships. They joined the audience seated in the hot open court, to watch this interesting match in the final set.

The slim, agile tennis player at the back of the court took a second out to wipe his face - his lovely, dark skin was shining from sweat. He scored a point and the Umpire called out 'Game Ensa'

'Hey, wait a minute ... that's Grandpa Dee's dad.

'What! We don't have any tennis players in our family.'

'Yes we did Mel; he used to be a tennis player here.'

'No way - he wanted to study Law.'

'I don't know about that ... but that's him!'

Judging by the scores of the final set, it looked like the other player could possibly win the match, but as the match went on, there was a ray of hope. It went to "tie break."

Granddad Ensa had broken the other player's serve to level the scores. The heat was on! Both players were now on par and it was his turn to serve. They battled on whilst the Umpire relayed the scores. '15 love, 15 all, 30:15; 30 all, 40:30; Deuce, Advantage Ensa.'

The boys jumped out of their seats; he only needed one more point to win the match.

'He's going to win,' they shouted. 'Come on Granddad - you can do it! You can win!'

But disappointedly, his scores fell back to "Deuce."

'Ah man!'

Then "Advantage".

'Yes!' They were jumping out of their seats again.

Then back to "Deuce".

'Oh come on! Why can't he just nail it?'

'Advantage Ensa,' the Umpire said again.

'Yes!' The boys jumped at least a foot in the air.

Everyone held their breath, waiting for him to nail it this time and to their relief; he did just that, by hitting a straight Ace right down the line like a Wimbledon Champ.'

'Game set and Match to Ensa,' declared the Umpire. The boys and the rest of the crowd jumped up from their seats and cheered 'Ensa! Ensa!'

Mikal discreetly picked up one of his tennis balls and slipped it into his pocket. Later, with the crowd still cheering, young Great Granddad Ensa lapped up the attention, whilst posing for the photographers.

Then he strolled proudly off the tennis court, looking quite handsome, with towel, bag and racket in hand; having absolutely no idea that he'd just being observed at his best, by his great grandsons.

Mikal grabbed Mel's arm. 'This is where he took the photo.' Mel looked blank. 'The photo Mel ... the one in the family album, he was posing exactly, the same and we have witnessed it.'

'Ahem ... glad you enjoyed it and figured out a few things. This is the second surprise we had in store for you,' said Elmstead.

'I knew that,' Mel said with a cheeky grin.

'No, you didn't, I was the one who figured it out!'

'No you didn't Mikal.'

'Yes I did.'

'Guys ... calm down! Let's not argue.'

The boys looked at him sternly. 'We weren't arguing!'

'Let's just call it a disagreement then,' said Birchard.

'Right ... it's time to go!' said Elmstead. 'We've kept our side of the bargain. You met your ancestors and saw all that you wanted to see in two countries.'

'Can we please watch the spring celebrations?'

'No Mikal, it's time to go!'

This time Birchard stepped in to negotiate indirectly. 'I wouldn't mind watching the spring celebrations for a bit, as long as we get back by yesterday's magic hour.'

'Fine ... have it your way Birchard! But if there's a problem, it's your call - game set and Match!'

As they got nearer to celebration grounds, the sound of music and strong drum beats filled the air, making Maskee jiggle in his leaf bag. There was a lovely aroma of Gambian food, and an appetising spread lined the tables, to match the appetites of all those attending.

Many people were feasting in the area, along with their Great Grandparents, who were busy chatting to friends - no doubt about the achievements of the day.

Mel and Mikal joined in, dancing "free-style" to the beat of the drums and instruments all around them.

'Hey would you two like to come and shake a leg?' Mikal beckoned to their magic trees.

'No thanks. We like to shake our leaves to the feel and sound of the wind,' replied Elmstead. 'That's so therapeutic!'

'Ok, suit yourselves,' Mikal replied.

They carried on dancing, pushing their way through the crowd. Suddenly, young Grandpa Dee and their Great Uncle Papis walked towards them, looking as young as they were. Mel and Mikal somehow guessed who they were as they continued walking.

Nanka Def,' they said, with a friendly smile.

The boys looked behind them, hoping that their greeting was directed to someone else, but their' eyes were on them. They had lost their invisible capes ... again!

'Haven't seen you before,' young Grandpa Dee said. 'Have you just moved here?'

'Our capes Mel!' Mikal cried out.

'Excuse me!' said Grandpa Dee. The boys were a bit surprised that he could speak English so well.

'Sorry ... we're just visiting from England,' they replied.

'Ah, you're two English boys,' said Uncle Papis. 'You English people like to say "sorry" or "pardon" for no particular reason. If you hang around us, we'll show you when you really need to say that.'

'You like to dance?' said Grandpa Dee.

'Yes, but we can't do your stuff,' replied Mel.

'Your stuff! It's not our dance - it is the fashion! Come,

let us show you how to do it.' As Mel and Mikal tried to copy their moves, their Great Grandparents came up behind them.

'We were wondering where you two had disappeared to,' said Great Grandpa Ensa. 'Who are these boys Papis?'

'We've just met them - they are from England.'

Mel did an introduction. 'I am Mel and this is Mikal Sir.'

'I see. What strange names you've been given.'

Mel smiled. 'We know; maybe you should tell our Grandpa that - he named us!'

Both boys pointed to Grandpa Dee and without thinking said 'He's right ...' then quickly paused.

'What was that?' said Great Granddad Ensa.

'Erm ... sorry, we meant that we'll be joining him soon,' said Mel.

'Have you just arrived for the celebrations with your parents? Great Grandma Yande asked with a smile similar to Grandpa Dee.

'No Ma'am, we came yesterday without them,' said Mel.

'Come and have some food and drinks with us,' said Grandpa Ensa. 'We Gambians are very welcoming you know.'

'We sort of gathered that,' Mikal said uneasily.

They ate and danced with their family, all the time wishing that they had their capes. Things were a lot easier when they had them on. Shortly after, they heard a new sound in the distance and decided to check it out.

'Excuse us,' they said to their relatives. 'We'll be back soon.'

They made their way through the crowd; moving nearer to the sound, when suddenly two weird looking creatures appeared from nowhere; spinning and dancing to the beat of the music.

They had limbs with leaves that rustled as they walked, sackcloth with slits for eyes and a mouth at the top end of their orange coloured trunks. It seemed like the creatures had singled the boys out from the crowd, because they started dancing wildly towards them and waving their sticks.

'Mel felt uneasy. 'I think I really need to pee,' he said crossing his legs.

'Come on let's run,' Mikal said suddenly.

Mel didn't need to be told twice. They started running, but so did the creatures. If they turned left, they followed.

If they turned right, they did the same and the crowd followed too. The boys were almost out of breath when they ended up cornered in a dead-end road and had to turn to face them. Eyeing them cautiously, they waited for their next move. Then one of them spoke -in English.

'Hey my brothers, why are you running? Don't you know that we Mandingos can out run most tribes?'

'What do you want?' said Mikal, suddenly acknowledging what he perhaps already knew that there was indeed a person masquerading behind the costume. One of them moved forward.

'Don't come any nearer,' said Mikal, 'If you try to harm us we'll ...we'll … call our magic trees.'

'That's right!' said Mel, backing him up.

'Hahaha, call your magic trees! Oh, we are really, really scared now,' one of them said. 'Listen, you boys are so stupid. We just wanted to challenge you to a dance, because you look like those tourists - you know - the westerners, especially in those weird clothes. Why do you let your fear get to you so?'

'Now he's beginning to sound like our magic trees,' said Mel. 'We dress weird, look who's talking! 'Why don't you take off your mask if you're so harmless?'

'We will ... after the celebration; but for now; we are dressed as Mandinka Masquerades.'

'Mandinka Masquerades!'

'Yes, this is an important part of some Gambian celebrations. 'If you were Gambians you'd recognise us by our costume and dance. Our speciality is the "Kankurang" dance.'

'Kan ... ku ... ra ....' stuttered Mel.

'Don't worry about the pronunciation, just come on; rise to our challenge and dance. We Gambians are some of the friendliest people in the world.'

The masquerades led them back to the main road. They did the basic steps of the Kankurang dance and signalled to the boys to join them, whilst the crowd clapped to spur them on.

The boys took up the challenge, but the moves were more difficult than those Grandpa Dee had shown them. Eventually they gave up, and challenged the Masquerades to compete with their modern, shuffle moves, and guess what; they could hardly keep up.

The crowd clapped, cheered and shouted for more.

Some even pushed the masquerades out of the way to copy their moves. It was interesting watching the women, who caught up in the excitement; outshone the men with their rhythm and dance steps.

The dancing continued for some time until finally, the boys were too exhausted to continue, so waving the crowd goodbye; they went in search of their capes and the trees.

'Great moves ...you've become stars!' said Birchard

'Oh that! Actually we were really worried at first,' said Mel.

'Yeah, yeah ... it's probably just a "fear" thing!' Birchard replied, as he winked at them and patted their backs.

Chapter 44: The Wild Chase

The aroma coming from the food tables left Mel and Mikal's mouths watering and they had a strong urge to sample the variety of dishes.

'Grandpa was right, the food is so delicious. Have you tried the peanut butter stew?' Mel asked and unexpectedly burped. 'Oh, excuse me!' Just then, he heard a low growl under the table and stooped down to look. 'Uh oh! Don't look now Mikal. They're two dogs under there like the ones at our uncle's house Talk about déjà vu, they can see us.'

The dogs poked their elongated mouths out from under the table and growled again. The boys did not hang around to see what would happen next; they grabbed a bottle of drink and started running. Unbelievably, the dogs chased after them like greyhounds on a racetrack; creating such a commotion that people stopped to stare at them and the drinks flying jerkily, through the air.

Some rushed out of the way of the wild chase, whilst the

drummers beat their drums faster to add to the confusion. Mel and Mikal took sharp turns to avoid the dogs nipping their rear end. Jumping onto a wall to escape the dogs, they lowered themselves onto a veranda. What they had not notice; were the steps leading to it from the gate.

Before they knew it, the dogs were in front of them growling as if to say, *'We've got you now!'* The boys backed up against the door of the house, and as the dogs moved steadily towards them, the door miraculously sprung open.

They tumbled in, scrambled to their feet and slammed the door in their faces, then headed for the back door. However, the clever dogs had sussed things out.

As the boys exited the back door, they were waiting. Mel imagined them saying with a growl in between each phrase, *'And now, finally, we've got you where we want you. You'd better not dare move … your T-shirts wouldn't be the only things we'd rip off.'*

They were trapped, but saw hope when two large gas-filled balloons with strings, from the celebration, floated above them. Mel and Mikal grabbed hold of a string each and surprisingly, the balloons floated above the wall with them in tow, as if they were carrying no extra weight.

They flew in the hot air, passing over fields that were so

dry; they looked like they were recovering from a drought. As they continued the flight out of the blue, a whizzing sound flew past their ears. The balloons were under attack from catapult stones; fired by boys below, who were totally, unaware of the invisible passengers attached.

To their dismay, the stones pierced the balloons and the air slowly, fizzled out as they drifted to the ground. Luckily, they landed in a row of bushes that helped to break their fall without sustaining any injuries; and picking themselves up, headed straight for the magic trees.

Below, Birchard was tackling the crazy dogs that were still barking near the back door of the house. His deep, Dart Vader-Optimus Prime tone, sounded just like before when he ordered the dogs back under the table.

With that sorted, it was time to leave. They had extended their stay, and sadly, there was no time to allow for goodbyes. The vortex appeared and took off in a flash of light to the amazement of the crowd.

Some were undoubtedly convinced that it was a sign from a heavenly presence; and you could say they were pretty close to the truth.

Chapter 45: Gifts, Flashbacks & Manuscript

Mel and Mikal returned to the garden, sadly acknowledging the fact that the last of their wishes had been fulfilled. Birchard and Elmstead would be sadly missed, also Maskee - the carved mask.

'Just don't go breathing on any other carving,' said Maskee. 'You wouldn't want another me around, because that might probably be my disagreeable twin.'

Descending from their branch seats, they said goodbye to Maskee, then hugged and thanked the magic trees for all the adventures. Those memories they felt would last forever.

'We've really had a great time,' said Mikal. 'My Biology and other Science lessons will never be the same again.'

'That is good - you are both going to be fine A* students.'

'There will be tears of joy instead of fear when we meet again Mel,' said Birchard, remembering their first encounter. 'But for now we must go swiftly.'

'Wait ... we forgot to ask about The Seer. Will we ever see him again?'

'Our Godlink, the Seer? He is of higher ranking as you might have already guessed. He told us about your great crystal ball adventure and it's possible that he'll visit again next summer, during one of our adventures.'

'Just remember not to confuse his voice with mine,' said Elmstead. 'It's horrendous, but I suppose you had noticed. Anyway, we have to go now. We were only meant to be with you boys for a short while. Come to the garden later for a final goodbye.'

Both trees embraced Mel and Mikal again before vanishing in a puff of air, leaving them to walk sadly back to their Grandparents' house. At the dining table, the boys were so full up with Gambian food and sadness that lunchtime for once was really a very sad, quiet affair.

Later, the boys discreetly placed the tennis ball and brooch near Grandpa Dee's CD player. He loved music and was always singing, at home at work, on stage, in his car, on the bus - you name it!

His children Andre, Kris and Keda always say, 'He can't

help himself, he just has to sing.'

Grandpa Dee felt puzzled when he saw his gifts. He examined the tennis ball engraved with "Gambian Tennis Championships" as if searching for clues. 'Where did this come from -who does it belong to?' he asked. 'My dad played tennis a long time ago with balls like this, but how did it get here?'

'Maybe some unknown entity brought it to you for good luck!' teased Grandma Cee.

He picked up the gold brooch. 'This looks so familiar. My mother lost a brooch like this many years ago. Look at it ... it is a genuine antique.'

'Exquisite!' said Grandma Cee

'Hang on a minute Cee, are you, or someone else playing tricks on me?'

'Playing tricks on you ... I don't have time for tricks! If you remember, the same thing happened to me - the doll, the handkerchief, the mangoes etc. It was as if they all fell out of the sky!'

'Grandpa, why don't you keep them? You could treat them as a "gift from the past" to remember your parents.'

'Well just like your Grandma, it's really a puzzle I'd like

to have solved, so whoever placed these things here, should own up.'

Mel decided to distract him, before it got out of hand. 'Can I ask you something Grandpa?'

'Yes, go ahead Mel.'

'Do you remember an incident in the school playground in Gambia, with bees from a tree?'

'Bees from a tree, oh yes I remember! I was there. How did you know about that?'

'I must have dreamt about it I guess.'

'You dreamt about it? Impossible! Your Grandma must have told you.'

'Don't look at me, you have never told me anything about bees at your school. Did they sting you?'

'No, I was lucky, but the children and myself, were so frightened, we all had to be sent home.'

'Really! So where did the bees come from?' Mel asked, as if he didn't know.

Grandpa Dee looked at Mel, and for a moment, it seemed like he was about to answer the question, but instead, he went on to say, 'I remember it like it was yesterday.'

'So do I Grandpa,' Mel muttered under his breath.

'Your Great Grandma Yande was so angry, but as usual kept her cool. They later took the elsewhere and cut down the tree, in case the bees returned.

'Did anyone every figure out who disturbed the bees, or did the person responsible own up?' Mel asked, hoping that he would confess.

'Well ... Well ...'

'Well what Grandpa?'

'I meant that no one owned up.' Grandpa Dee looked away with a hint of embarrassment in his eyes; then suddenly continued in a tone bursting with energy.

'But, luckily there was a celebration that afternoon with music and plenty of food. Everyone was there; mum, dad, my brother Papis and all the family, so we danced, ate, chatted and forgot about the bees.'

'I sort of remembered my brother Papis and I, dancing with two English boys, who disappeared in the crowd and never even came back to say goodbye. Come to think of it they were about your height, and their names sounded similar to yours; let me think now, Rel and Mica ... something like that.'

'That wasn't very polite,' said Mikal trying to keep a straight face. 'Maybe they were whisked off in a hurry by their guardians, before they had time to return.'

'Maybe, but there was also some sort of weird commotion with a couple of crazy dogs barking; bottles of drinks floating in the air and disappearing into a strange flash of light in the sky. I don't know what that was all about, so I just kept dancing. Some people had the crazy idea it was a sign that the end of the world was nigh.'

'Ah! Now that you have mentioned that Dee, I remember having a similar experience at my Great Grandparents' anniversary in Jamaica. Two boys popped up from nowhere as we were eating and said they were from the future - in the year 20 something -it seemed so far off at the time. I think they had similar names and were the same height as the ones you've just mentioned.'

'Really, how strange!' said Grandpa Dee.

'After they left,' Grandma Cee continued. 'I went to the water barrel at the side of the house, and there was this huge flash of light that nearly knocked me over. And, you know, I could have sworn I saw their faces in it before it totally disappeared.'

Mel and Mikal stood as stiff as a plank- they could not believe what they had just heard.

'You know what was funny; they said I was their Grandma; how ridiculous. I was only seven at the time. Also, they said that they liked my cake - can't remember which one, but it definitely wasn't rum cake - I had asked them about that.'

'Cee, did you put some of the rum for the cake in your ginger beer that day?' Grandpa Dee asked.

'No I did not,' Grandma Cee replied and playfully hit him with the newspaper. She took a step towards the dining table and suddenly remembered something. 'Carrot cake ....'

'What?'

'Carrot cake! They said they liked my carrot cake and fish pie ... but...' Grandma Cee turned to look at the boys.

'Hey...Cee, don't go speculating now. It was probably all a dream.'

'Well this dream was real, because my eyes and ears were wide opened.'

Mel and Mikal tried to keep a straight face, to hide their shock. She had come so close to sussing things out! Luckily, Grandpa Dee distracted her with his next statement.

He yawned, stretched his long slender legs under the table and said, 'Cee, those were the days eh!'

'They sure were,' she said, but her thoughts were still lingering on what she had just recalled from so long ago.

The boys breathed a sigh of relief and signalled to each other to meet up in the study, leaving their Grandparents reminiscing about their past.

'Can you believe it!' said Mel. 'She saw us ... she saw us take off! She not only saw us take off, she also remembered what we said.'

'Yeah, I nearly wet myself when she mentioned the carrot cake,' said Mikal.

Mel laughed. 'See, I'm not the only one!'

The manuscript was on the table once again and Mikal closed the door to have another peek. 'So Grandma's book is about a boy, no ... two boys. Huh! They are about our age!'

'Let me see Mikal. Elmstead said I would find it interesting. Mel flicked through the pages. 'What's this?' I don't believe it! I didn't think she could write scenes like this.'

'What? Where? Let's see!' said Mikal.

Mikal flicked through the pages again 'There's something here about a Croc... what's going on? Oh my days Mel! Do you think that her stories are about our advent ...?'

Mikal stopped in mid-sentence as he glanced at the door.

'Hey! What are you two doing in my study?' said Grandma Cee. 'Do you guys understand the word privacy?'

The boys apologised and left the study immediately. When they returned, the manuscript was nowhere to be seen. However, there were more pressing things to attend to, like their "goodbye meeting" with the trees. In their haste, they forgot about the manuscript, but no doubt, they will have the rest of the holidays and next summer to recall this.

I wonder if we'll have any more adventures with the trees?'

'I don't know,' Mikal replied in a lowered voice, obviously filled with sadness. 'They granted all our wishes, so maybe next time they'll let us make more.'

They stood quietly in the silence of the garden, looking at the magic trees that were firmly rooted next door. Their leaves swayed gently in the wind, with no sign of the powers displayed in their adventures. Mel smiled to himself as he reflected on how scary they were at first, especially, Birchard's tone.

'Well enjoy your vacation,' he said quietly. 'Don't forget to return next summer as promised.'

They turned to walk away with their heads hung low when there it was again - that familiar voice in the wind.

'We will noble buddies. Enjoy the rest of the summer and watch those T-shirts,' Birchard said with a faded giggle.

'See you next summer after our renewal,' said Elmstead, his voice also fading with the wind, but not before, he faintly recited:

'Alas my nobles the end of the summer is nigh, and now it's time for goodbyes and indeed a sigh Autumn our golden season draws near, and harsh winter months will leave us bare But destiny will ensure we meet again; for when the sun heats the sky, make your wish and to that, we will comply Farewell my nobles. Farewell!

'That was very poetic Elmstead!' said Mel.

'We knew you were a historian and a bit of a thespian,' said Mikal, 'but we didn't know you were a bit of a poet.'

'It's a new skill,' he replied in a voice even fainter than before. 'But, you guys shouldn't worry, because every little thing is gonna be alright.' He chuckled as the boys recognised the famous Bob Marley lyrics. 'See you next year, and as we always say boys, same time... same place! Treeie oh and Beh Chi Kanam!'

'I think that means "Goodbye" in Wolof or Jolof Mel.'

They walked back to the patio door, feeling much happier, having said their goodbyes once more to their now seemingly motionless, magical friends. 'Oh man, our lives will be boring once again Mel, but at least we won't get yelled at for getting our T-shirts dirty.'

'That's true, but I am going to miss travelling back in time and flying through the air in trees, vortex and balloons with invisible capes.'

'We won't get chased anymore by crocodiles, hyenas, dogs and Ratbats in caves,' said Mikal, 'or, peaceful Tainos. No getting caught up in a hurricane or a river that started out as a stream. No jumping off tree vines or in and out of 3D historical, movies through a crystal ball, and visually surfing through the earth's core.'

'There'll be no more boat rides; getting chased by Spanish ghosts, sleeping in hotels and trucks, and watching our aunt in a trance, whilst the magic trees sip green tea out of her china cups,' said Mel. 'That was soooo funny! No more talking to ghosts, magic masks and watching magic trees fight, before attending a grand ceremony.

No more, encounter with creepy lizards. And, oh yeah, I almost forgot Mel, no falling out of mango trees into another era, meeting an ancient female tree with trunk-coloured lipstick, and getting pelted with mangoes by green monkeys.'

'Come to think of it Mikal, it was really hilarious.'

'It wasn't at the time - cheeky monkeys! But hey, we have had a great summer adventure.

'Yep we sure did; can't wait to tell our friends!'

'Mel we promised the trees not to tell anyone about it, so we should keep our promise.'

'I suppose you're right. A promise is a promise - we have to keep it a secret!'

'Yeah ... a "safe kept" secret - got it!'

'That's very funny Mikal - you're improving!'

They started walking back towards the house and heard the rustling sound of the wind again, as if the trees approved. 'Look after yourselves noble buddies,' said Elmstead in a breezy whisper.

A really faint, Darth Vader-Optimus Prime voice said, 'We'll have a whale of a time next summer; so tek care, han walk good as the Jamaicans say.' With that, their voices totally faded into the silence of the garden.

'Goodbye,' the boys said quietly, waving one last time as they entered the dining room and closed the patio door; wondering what tomorrow will bring.

THE END - UNTIL NEXT TIME!

❧About the Author❧

Jamaican born, Cee Bennett-Carayol, has lived in England since her teenage years. She trained as a nurse after leaving school and later graduated from Middlesex and London Southbank University. Since then, she has worked in education as a professional Careers Guidance Practitioner, where she has had the pleasure of assisting many to achieve their goals.

Her interest in reading novels and writing stories developed from primary school, where reading was a regular pastime and was encouraged by her Aunt and Uncle. At school, she was always pleased, when her teacher sometimes found her stories interesting, to the extent that she shared them, with the rest of the class.

Her love for trees and nature in general is evident, especially amongst close family members. Incidentally, the inspiration for her debut novel came from an interesting tree, with wriggly leaves, hanging over her garden fence in Aylesbury, Buckinghamshire.

Other inspirational sources came from her clever grandsons, who the main characters of the novel are based on, along with her children and amazing family members, whom she shared a home with, in her younger years.

WATCH OUT FOR THE SEQUEL, "THE MAGIC RETURNS!"

.